BLURRED LINES

A RIXON HIGH PREQUEL

L A COTTON

Published by Delesty Books

BLURRED LINES

Copyright © L A Cotton 2021
All rights reserved.

Edited by Andrea M Long
Proofread by Sisters Get Lit(erary) Author Services
Cover Designed by Lianne Cotton
Image: CJC Photography

CHAPTER ONE

Avery

"AVERY, let's go. You're going to be late," Dad yelled.

"I'll be right down." He didn't need to know I was still only half-dressed.

It was the first day of senior year and I was late.

Fuck my life.

My door swung open and my sister Ashleigh grinned. "Hey, liar."

"Get out, brat."

"Dad's going to kill you when he realizes you're not even dressed." She flashed me a saccharine smile.

"We can't all be like you, Leigh."

Little Miss Perfect poked her tongue out at me. "You're a jackass."

"And you're annoying as fuck. Now go, get out of here. If you loved me, you'd go downstairs and buy me five minutes with Dad."

"Yeah, whatever." She pulled the door shut and I let out a sigh of relief.

It was her first day of ninth grade which meant she was starting Rixon High School.

Mom and Dad wanted us to eat breakfast together and then take photos. It was totally embarrassing. But in the Chase family, you didn't get to be embarrassed. Uncle Xander was probably downstairs too, here to watch the show.

"Avery, don't make me come up there," Dad yelled.

"Fuck," I muttered, shoving some gel through my dark blond hair.

It was senior year; I had a lot riding on the next few weeks.

Grabbing my backpack and gym bag, I finally left my bedroom and made my way downstairs. Sure enough, Uncle Xander was already seated at the table, wolfing down a stack of pancakes.

"Here he is, the man of the hour," he teased, and I flipped him off. "Big year ahead."

"Sit." Mom grabbed my shoulders and kissed my cheek. "Eat."

"I'm not—"

"I said eat."

"Do what your mother said, Son. It's one morning. That's all we ask."

"Yeah, whatever." I dropped into the chair opposite Ashleigh and she smirked.

"Brat," I mouthed.

"Asshole."

Laughter rumbled in Xander's chest. He was my uncle, sure, but I'd grown up with him. He'd finally moved out a couple of years ago, and the house just wasn't the same. He still came over all the time though. Mostly to eat or if he needed some money.

"A senior." Mom placed down some pancakes. "I can't believe it. It doesn't seem five seconds since your dad and I were seniors." She gazed longingly at him and he stopped what he was doing and stalked toward her.

Ashleigh sighed dreamily, a huge fan of their public displays of affection. I, on the other hand, fake barfed all over my breakfast.

"Hey, knock it off." Dad pinned me with a dark look. "One day a special girl will knock you off your feet, Son, and then—"

"Yeah, yeah, save me the speech, Dad." I'd heard it all before. "It's senior year. I don't have time for girls."

The truth was, there was only one girl I'd ever wanted, and I'd spent the last few months avoiding her like the plague.

"Hear fucking hear," Xander said around a mouthful of pancakes. Dad didn't even bother reprimanding him for cussing anymore. Xander had issues. A whole heap of them. But he was family.

And as my parents liked to remind me all the time, there was nothing more important.

"It's good to have focus, baby." Mom brought me a glass of juice. "But remember to have a little fun too. It's senior year. After this, everything changes."

She didn't need to remind me. The huge pit in my stomach was reminder enough. It had grown over the last couple of weeks, shifting and stretching until I felt hollow.

It was senior year, my time to shine. My time to show every scout, every coach and team, every fan why I was the captain of the Rixon Raiders.

"You okay, Son?" Dad's voice pulled me from my thoughts.

"Uh, yeah." I got up and took my plate to the sink.

"Everything you've worked for over the past few years all boils down to this moment."

"I know, Dad." My eyes lifted to his, and the pride shining there weighed heavily on my chest. I wasn't just carrying my hopes for the future, I was carrying his.

"You're going to go all the way, Avery. I feel it in my bones."

"Cam." Mom gave him a stern look and he backed away, but not before winking at me and mouthing, "You got this."

"Come here, baby." She pulled me in, holding me at arm's length. "Let me get a look at you. God, I remember when you were born. So tiny and wriggly. And you made this little bleating sound." Tears filled the corners of her eyes. "I'm proud of you, Avery." She pulled me in and hugged me tight. "Whatever you decide to do, I'm proud of you."

"Jeez, give the kid some room." Xander huffed. "He's starting senior year, not going off to war."

"Very helpful, thanks, Xan." Dad scolded him. The two of them fought like cats and dogs these days, but I knew it was only because Dad was worried.

We all were.

"Ashleigh, get over here with your brother. I want to take a photo."

"Mom, do we have to?" I protested.

"Humor me. This is your last 'first day of high school,' baby."

When she put it like that...

Hooking my arm around my sister, I yanked her in and ruffled her hair. "Smile for the camera, brat."

"Go duck yourself, jackass."

"Hey hey," Dad said. "Enough already. Now get out of here or you're going to be late. Avery, walk with me." He motioned toward the hall and I grabbed my bags, following him.

"What's up, Dad?"

"I want you to promise me you'll look out for Ashleigh and Lily this year."

"Dad, come on... It's senior year. I can't do—"

"Ashleigh is strong, she's got this. But Lily is... well, after what happened, she's struggling. Just be a friend, okay."

Lily was Ashleigh's best friend. She was also my dad's best friend's daughter. He was kind of a big deal in Rixon.

He was also my coach.

"Fine, but I'm not babysitting." I had a full plate as it was.

"Nobody is asking you to. Just keep an eye on

them, and if you get wind of any... issues, you go straight to Jase with that shit, okay?"

"Yeah, okay."

He nodded. "You're a good kid, Avery. Now get out of here. And drive safely. Your sister is precious cargo."

———

"OKAY, brat, tell me the rules again."

"Avery, come on," Ashleigh whined. "I'm not doing this."

"Tell me, or else I'll tell dad you were trying to flirt with my guys... again."

"I was not flirting. I was having a conversation."

"I saw you batting your eyelashes and twirling your hair at Micah."

"Micah? Gross."

I arched a brow. "You think Micah is gross? That's not what I heard you telling Poppy and Sophia."

"I—" Her cheeks flushed beet red.

"Yeah, that's what I thought." I smirked. "Just make sure it's only gossiping you're doing. My guys are off-limits."

"I'm in ninth grade, jackass. Your guys wouldn't

look twice at me, and besides, if they ever did, Dad and Uncle Xan would kick their asses all the way to State if they found out."

"Damn right they would. But don't be mistaken... the rule doesn't only apply to my guys; it applies to guys period."

"Whatever. Just because you're a manwhore of epic proportions doesn't mean the rest of us want to be."

"Jesus, Leigh, I'm not—"

"How many girls did you sleep with over the summer?"

What the actual fuck?

"I am not having this conversation with you," I gritted out. "I think I see Lily. You should probably go find her."

"Nice diversion tactic, jackass."

"Get out of here, Ash," I chuckled, but she leaned over and punched my arm.

"You are so freaking annoying." She hated it when people called her Ash, because my dad's other best friend was called Asher and that was his nickname. Instead, she made us call her Leigh, which I did, unless I was in tease mode.

"Takes one to know one," I called after her as I climbed out of my car.

My sister headed straight for Coach Ford's daughters. Lily and Poppy were a grade apart, but it wasn't the only thing separating them. Lily was all her father, dark hair and icy blue eyes that looked right through you. But Poppy, she was her mom. Wavy brown hair and green eyes and a smile that lit up like the fourth of July. We'd all grown up together: me and Ashleigh; the Ford girls; Sofia and Aaron, the Bennet twins, and later their foster brother Ezra. But because I was the eldest, and three years older than Ashleigh, Lily, and Ezra, I wasn't as tight with them.

"Yo, Chase," Micah and Ben made their way over.

"What's up?" I said.

"Senior year, man. We're gonna rule the school and dominate the field this season."

"Fuck, yeah," Ben said, fist bumping Micah. "You good?" he asked me. "You look stressed."

"I'm chill." My shoulders lifted in a small shrug. "Not looking forward to getting back in the gym though."

Our regime would be brutal this year. After a crushing defeat last season, we'd missed out on the championship game. As captain and quarterback, it was a bitter pill to swallow. The season should have been ours. But a string of injuries had upset our flow.

"Seriously?" Ben balked. "I can't wait. Nothing like a few reps to get the blood pumping."

We walked toward the school building. Guys stopped to say 'hey' or high five us and girls paused to smile and bat their eyelashes. We weren't just seniors this year. We were fucking kings... and the empire rested squarely on my shoulders.

I had to take them to State. I had to bring home the championship. I had to catch the eye of a scout to one of my preferred colleges.

It was a lot, and as we walked into school, I knew it was only about to get a hell of a lot worse.

"Snitch alert." Micah coughed into his hand as we passed Miley Fuller. She caught my eye and went to speak, but I shot her a cold glare and kept walking.

She was the last person I wanted to talk to.

"I can't believe she has the balls to come back here."

"Seriously, bro, she goes here." Ben snorted. "What was she going to do, leave?"

"Uh, hell yeah. After what she did, I'm surprised her parents didn't haul her out of Rixon High and send her to juvie."

"You don't just get sent to juvie, man. That's not

how it works. Besides, she didn't actually commit a crime."

"Try telling that to Coach and the team. Hey, what says you, Chase?"

I glanced up at them and shrugged. "Doesn't matter."

"Doesn't matter?" Micah's brows hit his hairline. "The backstabbing bitch spent the entire season posing as a cheerleader to get the scoop on the team and then wrote that story for the school newspaper."

"Micah, I said drop it." I didn't want to talk about Miley and her lies... her betrayal.

I didn't want to talk about her at all.

"What's up your ass, bro?"

I slammed my locker shut and ran a hand through my hair. "I gotta get to class. I'll see you guys later."

But as I stalked off down the hall and rounded the corner, Miley intercepted me.

"Can we talk?" Her eyes darted around me. "Please."

"I think you said everything you needed to say in your article." My teeth ground together as her soft tawny eyes silently pleaded with me.

"I know I messed up, Ave, and I'm so sor—"

"Don't call me that. Only friends get to call me that, and you and me, Fuller, we're not friends."

We were nothing.

"But—"

I stepped up to her, the hitch of her breath barely affecting the ice around my heart. "Get the fuck out of my way," I hissed, "and if you know what's good for you, you'll stay out of it."

CHAPTER TWO

Miley

AVERY SHOULDERED PAST ME, taking off down the hall as if he couldn't stand to be around me a second longer.

I didn't blame him.

I'd really messed up junior year. At the beginning of the semester, Mr. Jones had informed the three junior reporters that he wanted us to compete for the head editor's position. I'd wanted it. I'd wanted it so freaking bad. I knew I'd need to break a story that got attention. I just hadn't anticipated it would break my heart too.

I let out a resigned sigh and moved down the hall

to my locker. A couple of cheerleaders shot me a death glare.

I hadn't only pissed off the football players.

At the time, I'd been laser focused on my end goal—becoming head editor this year. Nothing else had mattered... until it did.

I'd never been a football fan. I loved words: literature and books. I loved using the power of language to express myself. I didn't have time for team sports, not when I had my hopes set on Northwestern. You needed to give your all to academia, to hone your craft and develop your voice as a writer.

And the exposé on the truth about football players and the preferential treatment they received had won me the position. But it came at a cost.

One I hadn't anticipated.

Once I'd added some books to my locker, I hitched my bag up my shoulder and headed for class.

The second I stepped inside the room though, I internally winced. Micah Delfine and Ben Chasterly were in this class. And they were in the thick of a group of cheerleaders.

Just what I didn't need.

"Miss Fuller, don't make me wait all day," the teacher said. "Find a seat."

"Sorry, sir." I hurried to an empty chair over by the window.

"Snitch bitch." Someone coughed, but the words rang out clear.

I sucked in a ragged breath, trying not to let their taunts and jibes hurt. I deserved it, mostly. I guess I just thought summer vacation would make people forget.

But no one forgot in a place like Rixon. Especially, where their beloved football team was involved. Because Rixon wasn't just any town; it was a football town, and the Rixon Raiders was one of the best teams in state.

And I was the girl who went against them for her own gain.

———

BY THE TIME class was over, I was more than ready to get out of there. The constant whispers and notes had been insufferable. It was a new year, a new semester, but nobody had forgotten about the girl who infiltrated the cheerleading squad to get close to the football team and write an undercover article for the school newspaper.

I'd joined the stream of kids leaving the room,

when someone yanked me back. "Watch it, bitch," Kendall Novak said as she shouldered past me, her girlfriends all following in her footsteps.

I'd never been a popular kid. I'd never sat with the cool kids at lunch or been invited to the best parties, but I'd never been so ostracized by my peers before. *You only have yourself to blame.*

I couldn't take back what I'd done. I couldn't even regret it. It had stood out against the competition and landed me the head editor's position.

I'd got what I wanted... hadn't I?

At least I didn't have to spend the next hour listening to my classmates seriously low opinions of me. I had a free period and there was one place I wanted to be.

The second I walked into the Rixon Riot HQ— also known as a small room next to the library—I felt a calm wash over me. This was my calling, my safe space. Behind these doors, nothing my peers said about me could touch me.

"Morning, Mil," Dexter Palmer, my second-in-command, smiled. "How was the jungle this morning?"

"I survived." Barely.

"Well, Jones is in his office and he wants to talk." His brows went up.

I dumped my bag and grabbed a notebook and pen. "Guess I'd better go see what he wants."

Making my way over to the office in the corner of the room, I knocked twice.

"Come in," Mr. Jones called, and I slipped inside. "Miley, welcome back."

"Thanks, sir."

He motioned to the empty seat and I sat down. "Senior year, are you ready?"

"I think so."

"Good, I'm excited to see what you'll bring to the role this year." He ran his eyes over the computer screen. "I have your first project."

"You do?" A lick of excitement trickled through me.

"Coach Ford would like you to shadow the team this semester and—"

"I'm sorry, what?" The excitement turned to ice.

"Hear me out." Mr. Jones sat back in his chair and steepled his fingers. "The article was a big success and has already raised some interesting points that Principal Kiln plans to take to the school board, but it also ruffled a lot of feathers."

"That was kind of the point, sir." Like many

schools, Rixon High had a history of giving its athletes preferential treatment.

"I know, and you know I support most of the points you raised in your piece. But with these kinds of exposés there is always a backlash. And it's a big season for the team. Coach Ford would like you to shadow one of their star players to understand the pressure they're under."

"You're serious?"

"I am." His brows knitted. "And so is Principal Kiln."

"So I don't have a choice?"

"This is a great opportunity, Miley. As investigative journalists we have to be prepared to look at all sides of the story. I know you can do this."

"The team won't want me hanging around."

They hated me.

"Well, it isn't their call to make. Coach Ford wants this piece to happen. He'll make sure his players fall in line."

"Great." Sarcasm coated my voice.

"I'm sure you'll figure it out," he said around a half-smile. "Your tenacity and dedication to the newspaper is second-to-none."

"Thank you, sir. I guess I'd better go and prepare." I grabbed my bag and stood up.

"Don't you want to know who you'll be shadowing?"

"Doesn't matter." My shoulders lifted in a small shrug.

"Actually, it might..."

My eyes locked on his, the knot in my stomach tightening.

And then he said three little words that tipped my world on its axis.

"It's Avery Chase."

———

"MILEY, IS THAT YOU, SWEETHEART?"

"It's me, Mom." I smiled to myself. We didn't get a lot of visitors, but she asked the same question every single day.

After kicking off my sneakers, I went to find her in the kitchen. "Hey."

"Hey, sweetheart. Good 'last first day?'"

"It was okay." Thankfully, she couldn't see my grimace as I went to the refrigerator and pulled out a juice box. I stabbed the straw into the top and joined her over by the counter. "What are you making?"

"Reese's brownies."

"Hmm, my favorite."

"I thought we could have a movie night. Celebrate your first day of senior year."

"Sounds great, Mom. But I have a ton of reading to do. Later?"

"Sure, baby. Did you see Mr. Jones? Does he have a big senior year story for you?"

"He wants me to shadow Avery Chase."

"The quarterback?"

"That's the one." I couldn't keep the frustration out of my voice.

"But you already did the article on the team."

"And Coach Ford thinks it's only fair I do something reflecting them in a better light."

"Well, that doesn't seem very fair."

"In case you didn't know, life isn't fair, Mom." The second I said the words, I felt like crap. "I'm sorry, that came out wrong."

"It's okay, baby." She came around and hugged me. "I never want you to feel like you can't use me as a sounding board, okay? Whatever it is."

"Thank you."

It had been a rough couple of years. My dad walked out on us suddenly after twenty years of marriage to my mom. He'd said they had 'moved in different directions' but we both knew he'd found happiness with a woman only a few years older than me.

Mom had really struggled at first, falling into a bout of depression and anxiety. But she was doing better, and I was so damn proud of her for bouncing back.

"You'll ace it, sweetheart." She squeezed my hand. "I have no doubt. How was your first day besides that?"

I couldn't hide my frown this time.

"Ugh, that bad?"

"I'm head of the school newspaper, Mom. I wrote an exposé uncovering the preferential treatment of football players in our school. I tried out for the cheer squad just to get the inside scoop and—"

"Okay, okay, I get it. You broke a lot of people's trust, but surely, many are on your side?"

"Oh, I'm not sure about that." At our daily briefing half my team hadn't even been able to look me in the eye.

I was the girl who dared to go up against the Rixon Raiders, and now I had to pay the price.

"Well, you're a strong, independent woman." She nudged my shoulder. "There's nothing you can't handle."

"Yeah," I murmured, really wanting to move on from this conversation.

It was bad enough I had to do it all again tomorrow, but shadowing Avery for the article?

He was never going to agree to that.

Mom was right though. I wasn't one to back down from a challenge and I still needed my last submission piece for my application to Northwestern. I'd been mulling over ideas for the last couple of weeks, but this would have to do. I was too close to give up now, and I had too much riding on this semester as head editor at The Rixon Riot.

"That had better not be a frown, Miley Louise Fuller." Mom smiled, offering me a spoonful of brownie mixture. It was times like these, I realized how far she'd come.

After Dad left, she'd spent most of her days in bed, barely eating or drinking. It had been hard, watching the woman who had given me life fall to pieces like that. It was enough to sever my relationship with my father... but it had also made me more determined than ever to chase my dreams and carve out a future for myself.

Northwestern was the goal. I didn't have a plan b or c. It was one of the best writing programs in the country and I wanted it with every fiber of my being.

They only gave a handful of full academic scholarships every year and I needed one to be able to afford the tuition. Mom didn't have the money and my part-time job at Rixon's library wasn't enough.

"I've got this, Mom," I said with conviction. Because there was no alternative. She was right. I was Miley Louise Fuller, and when I set my sights on something—willingly or not—I went after it with everything I had. So regardless of whether Avery wanted to work with me on this or not, he had no choice.

Because I wouldn't give him one.

CHAPTER THREE

Avery

IT WAS ONLY the second day of the semester and all the telltale signs of the impending football season were everywhere. The huge Rixon Raiders banner hanging from the ceiling, the Viking mascot watching over me and my classmates like an all-seeing god. It was the same mascot my dad and Coach Ford had played to. Prayed to.

They'd ruled the halls of this very school over twenty years ago. Coach Ford had gone all the way, having a successful college career at UPenn and then drafting to the Philadelphia Eagles. But not my dad; he'd dropped out of college in senior year to take care of Xander when my grams got sick. Then Mom found out she was pregnant with me, and he'd given up his shot at going pro—and he'd had a good shot too—for family. He said he didn't regret it, but I figured that was what he was supposed to say. Going pro was a dream, one not many guys got to live out. So to give that up... I couldn't even imagine.

I wanted it more than I wanted anything else in the world. Football was a part of me, the way oxygen was a part of my blood. When I held a football, cradled the pigskin in my fingers, I felt at peace. It wasn't something you could put into words: the thrill of the game, the all-consuming high that came with running play after play. I'd lived and breathed football ever since I was just a toddler running around the yard being chased by Uncle Xander. My old man hoped I'd be a wide receiver like he was, but it quickly became apparent that throwing was my superpower. It became a standing joke between my dad and Coach Ford, that I should have been his son. It didn't matter though because as soon as I started Rixon High, I became his protégé. He took me under his wing and nurtured me into the player I was today.

A player with his eye on the prize. That prize being a full ride to one of the best programs in the country, Notre Dame.

"Chase, son, let's go." Coach Ford yelled as I pulled on my jersey. We'd been conditioning for the last hour and I was in desperate need of a shower, but after Miley Fuller's article last year, Coach had informed us he expected us to pull our weight in class as much as on the field. We all knew he was probably taking heat from Principal Kiln, but he didn't say it.

Coach Ford was a man of few words. Unless he was pissed, and then you felt the full wrath of his vocabulary.

"What's up, Coach?" I slipped into his office and closed the door.

"Take a seat, Avery."

"Sounds serious."

"Before I lay this out for you, I want you to know it was my idea. Mine, okay?"

"Okay." My brows pinched.

He sat back in his chair and let out a heavy sigh. "After the shitshow that was Miss Fuller's exposé, it brought heat onto the team that quite frankly we could do without this season. It's a big year for you. I don't want you distracted or having to jump through hoops..."

"Why don't I like the sound of this?" I shifted uncomfortably on the chair.

"I spoke to Mr. Jones—"

"The Rixon Riot teacher?"

Coach nodded. "And he agreed that we should get a fair and equal shot at telling our side of the story. It's no secret that athletes get preferential treatment. Especially in a town like Rixon, and most of the parents are on our side, you know that. But I can't ignore the fact that it didn't paint us—me—in the best light."

"Mrs. Bennet breathing down your neck still?" Sofia and Aaron's mom was the guidance counselor at school and a firm believer in academics first and sports second. She and Coach often butted heads over players schedules and grades. The exposé was only more ammunition.

"Mya knows the deal. I'm here to mold you into college players. I'm here to play football."

"Me too, Coach." I smirked.

"Yeah, well. You need to graduate high school too, son."

"My GPA is decent."

"So let's keep it that way. Anyway, back to my original reason for dragging you in here. I've agreed with Mr. Jones that Miss Fuller can come back and write another story."

"What the fuck?"

Coach's brow shot up and I let out a frustrated sigh.

"Sorry."

"I know you've got better things to be doing than babysitting the wannabe reporter."

"Whoa, you didn't say anything about babysitting her."

"Didn't I? Must have slipped my mind." He grinned. Coach actually grinned. "She's going to shadow you and you're going to show her the real truth behind the team."

"I am?" Like hell I was. She was a snake who couldn't be trusted. "How do we know she won't spin the story again?"

"Mr. Jones assures me Miss Fuller will be more than amiable."

"I bet he did," I grumbled.

"This is a good thing, Avery. Shining the light on you this season is exactly the kind of attention we need if we want Notre Dame to come knocking."

Fuck. He had to go and throw in that curveball.

"You really think we can trust her?"

"I'm sure you'll win her over. We're football players, not monsters."

"I don't know, Micah is pretty scary on the field."

29

He was our defensive tackle, and the guy was built like a brick house.

"Come on, Ave. Where's that fighting spirit?"

That was the thing though, it was senior year and I felt... off-kilter. I couldn't explain it. I'd had a fucking epic summer hanging with friends, attending football camp, and goofing around down at the lake. But as the days ran out and senior year crept closer, I began to feel restless. Maybe it was the pressure. Or maybe it was the fact my dad still thought I was planning to apply to Michigan and attend his alma mater.

"You still haven't told him?" Coach Ford pinned me with a knowing look.

"It didn't come up."

"Shit, Avery, you had the entire summer."

"I know but he's just so damn excited about Michigan. I don't know how to take that away from him." He'd sacrificed his dream for his family, but now he had the chance to live it vicariously through me.

"You're lucky I've been preoccupied, or there's a good chance I would have slipped it out by now."

"How is she?" I asked.

Coach let out a heavy sigh as he rubbed his jaw. "Lily is strong. Stronger than she gives herself credit for. But I'd be lying if I said I don't worry about high school. I thought middle schoolers were something else, but these high school girls... they can be brutal."

He wasn't wrong there.

"I'll keep an eye out. And she has Poppy and Ashleigh."

Poppy was still in junior high, but she was fiercely protective of her big sister. Coach had his hands full of females. Sometimes I wondered how he did it. But Jason Ford was one of the strongest guys I knew, and he loved his family something fierce.

"I'd really appreciate that, Avery. She's been through too much already."

"You got it, Coach." I nodded. I'd given my dad shit about it, but I would never turn a blind eye to someone making Lily's life any harder than it needed to be. She was as good as family.

"So you good with this Miss Fuller thing? I know it's not what you wanted to hear, but honestly, I think it could be a good thing."

My jaw clenched as I imagined spending time with her again. "I guess I don't have much of a choice, do I?"

The faintest of smirks traced Coach's lips. "That's the spirit."

———

I DIDN'T WAIT for Miley to hunt me down. Instead, I decided to take matters into my own hands. If we were going to do this thing, and it didn't seem like I had much choice, I was going to make sure she understood it was going to happen my way.

One of the tech guys managed to find me her schedule, so I waited outside her final class of the day. Everyone spilled into the hall, the teacher following them, but there was no sign of Miley.

Poking my head around the door, I found her packing up her things.

"Avery?" Even my name on her lips annoyed me.

"We need to talk." I closed the door and approached her.

"Coach told you about the article?" I nodded, and her cheeks pinked. "It wasn't my idea, I swear."

"Doesn't matter." Retrieving the scrap of paper from my pocket I slammed it down on her desk. "This is my schedule. Be there, or don't, whatever. But this is what you get."

I turned to walk away, but Miley reached across the desk and snagged my wrist. "Wait, please."

My eyes locked on to where she was touching me, anger boiling in my veins. "Get your fucking hand off me." It was a low growl that had her instantly releasing me.

"I'm sorry, okay? I know I messed up... but you don't understand. This is my life, my future—"

"You think I care?" I snapped. "I don't. But mess with me again, mess with my team again, and we will have a fucking problem, got it?"

Apology and regret glittered in her eyes and I hated it.

I hated her.

I wasn't typically an asshole. I didn't abuse my position, or the power bestowed to me by my team and our fans. But Miley Fuller made me real fucking angry.

Marching to the door, I expected her to let me go. But she was a reporter. It wasn't in her nature to stay silent.

"For what it's worth, Avery... I never meant for it to go down like that."

I didn't spare her a second glance as I ripped the door open and got the fuck out of there.

———

"WHAT CRAWLED up your ass and died?" Ashleigh asked the second I reached my car. I'd promised her a ride home. I didn't remember extending that offer to Lily.

I ignored her question, running my eyes over Ashleigh and her friend. "I'm not a taxicab."

"Maybe I should just wait for my dad," Lily said, and I felt like a proper shithead.

"Get in," I said. "It's no bother to give you a ride."

"O-okay."

Shaking my head, I climbed inside and waited for them. Lily burrowed into the door as if she was trying to shield herself. I'd seen her around the halls at school. She kept to herself, trying to blend into the shadows. It was a real fucking shame too. I remembered her as a kid. She'd always been so happy, so warm and kind. But that all changed in the summer before eighth grade.

Coach wasn't wrong when he said middle schoolers were something else.

"So how are you finding high school?" I asked as I backed out of the parking lot.

"I'm just relieved to be out of Rixon Middle," Ashleigh said.

"Lily?" I coaxed and she met my gaze in the rearview, but quickly averted her eyes.

"I-it's okay, I guess."

"You've got this, Lil." Ashleigh flashed her a warm smile. "So back to my original question, brother of mine. What crawled up your ass and died?"

"Nothing." I shrugged, keeping my eyes ahead.

"You are such a liar. I'm your sister. I know when something's up, and you stormed out of school like you couldn't be in there a second longer."

"Just leave it, yeah, Leigh?"

Her eyes drilled holes into the side of my face, but I wasn't about to confess.

I had bigger problems.

Like telling my dad I wanted to go to Notre Dame.

CHAPTER FOUR

Miley

WEDNESDAY MORNING BEFORE CLASSES, I found myself sitting on the bleachers, watching as Avery and the team ran drills. My reusable coffee cup warmed my hands as I observed Coach bark orders at them as they zipped up and down the field. Growing up, I'd never been a football fan. I was too busy losing myself in the fantastical worlds of the authors I loved so much. I was and always would be a bookworm, preferring to curl up on a chair at home or in the library, escaping to some faraway land.

So the fact anyone wanted to drag themselves out on a football field at half past seven in the morning and get pummeled by each other, running their legs to jelly, was beyond me. But I couldn't deny the dedication of these young men. The same young men I'd watched last year party too hard, miss assignment deadlines, and exploit the power bestowed on them all because they could throw a football, or tackle a guy their size to the ground.

Sure, I'd seen them run drills and play games. I'd been a cheerleader for the season, so it kind of came with the territory. But this was different. This was seeing it through new eyes.

"Okay, ladies, gather round." Coach Ford's voice boomed across the field. He was an intimidating man: all cool gaze, with a layer of scruff on his jaw, and a physique that most of the female teachers around school got tongue-tied over whenever they saw him. He was also NFL royalty, so he was kind of a big deal in a small town like Rixon.

I noticed Lily Ford, his daughter, sitting down a few rows, also watching. She'd just started Rixon High, but from what I could tell, she was a shy little thing, which seemed odd for the coach's daughter. Usually, girls flaunted their connection to the team. Sister, friend, ex... booty call; girls wore their connection to the team like a badge of honor. But the daughter of one of the Philadelphia Eagles' best players ever looked like she was trying to disappear.

I contemplated going down there, introducing myself. But something stopped me.

Specifically, Avery hollering my name across the field.

What the hell was he doing?

"Let's go, Fuller, get down here." He beckoned me over and reluctantly, I got up and traipsed over to where the team were huddled. Coach Ford gave me a sharp nod.

"We figured if you're going to be shadowing the team, the least you could do is make yourself useful." Avery smirked, throwing a ball at me. I fumbled it but managed to snatch it close to my body.

"I'm sorry, what?"

"You're not going to learn much from up there." He flicked his head to the bleachers. "You want to know what it's like to be a football player, don't you?" His eyes pinned me to the spot, and I felt my cheeks flush.

He thought he was so damn smart embarrassing me in front of the rest of the team.

"What Avery is trying to say," there was a warning in Coach Ford's voice, "is that we thought you might like to watch from the sideline."

"I can do that," I said, throwing the ball back at Avery without warning. He didn't see it coming and fumbled the catch. A couple of the guys laughed, but their captain silenced them with a deadly glare.

"Okay, okay. Miss Fuller, you're with me," Coach Ford said. "Ladies, let's show her how we play ball.

I followed Coach to the sideline area. "You good?" he asked me.

"I can handle the likes of Avery Chase," I scoffed, indignation burning through me.

He wanted to embarrass me, to make me feel stupid in front of his teammates. Part of me didn't blame him, but I also didn't expect it from him.

Not the Avery Chase I'd spent last season watching lead the team to the state championship.

Avery was levelheaded, calm, and composed. He didn't lose his head like Micah Delfine or Ben Chasterly. He was a firm, but fair captain who led by example. He didn't let his emotions get the better of him... until now.

Coach Ford folded his arms over his broad chest and chuckled. "Oh, I don't doubt it for a second, Miss Ful—"

"Miley. You can call me Miley."

"Very well, Miley. He's a good kid, you know. One of the best players I've had the privilege of working with."

"You think he can go all the way?"

"Oh, I know he can. But the hard work is only just starting. You want to go to college, Miley?"

"Northwestern, sir." God, I didn't just want it. I yearned for it.

"And what would you do to get there?"

"Whatever it takes, sir."

He regarded me for a long second, and I felt my stomach knot under the weight of his stare. "Then I guess you and my players aren't that different, after all. Something to think about."

Coach Ford excused himself and left me with my thoughts. I'd been so consumed last year with the article, that maybe I'd been too hasty in my conclusions. I still believed that being an athlete didn't entitle you to play the system. Because an education was just as important, and the reality was most of these players wouldn't end up with a professional career in football. But maybe I had first underestimated the power of sportsmanship, teamwork, and dedication.

Maybe.

———

I SPENT the next couple of days balancing classes and my responsibilities at the school newspaper, alongside shadowing Avery at practice. Most of the guys ignored me as if I wasn't there, and Avery barely spoke two words to me. But I wasn't there to make friends. I was there to write a kickass article and finish my submission for Northwestern.

"Oh look, it's the snitch." Kendall and her friends crowded me in class again. I glanced up at her and let out a heavy sigh.

"Very original."

"I heard you're sniffing around the team again. I didn't realize they let traitors hang out at practice."

"And what do we have here?" Micah strolled up to us, slinging his arm around Kendall's shoulder.

"Is it true she's writing another article?"

"Article? No way. We have much better uses for the snitch this year. Isn't that right, Miley?" He smirked at me. "She's our new mascot if you will."

"Yeah," Ben chuckled, elbowing his friend in the rib. "The team's very own stress reliever."

"Gross," I muttered, trying to ignore the girls' snickers.

"We're taking bets on how many Rixon dicks she'll suck before the season is out."

"I wouldn't touch you if you were the last guy on the planet."

"Ouch, you say that like you have other options. Do you... have other options? Because I don't think I've ever seen you with a friend, let alone a guy."

I swallowed down the wave of embarrassment crashing inside of me. So I didn't have many friends. I liked my own company. And between school, my part-time job, and spending time with Mom, there wasn't exactly time to date.

Not that I had a queue of guys knocking at my door.

"Oh my God, how sad," Kendall said. "She's a loner and a snitch. Sucks to be you."

"Okay, people take your seats." The teacher finally arrived, ushering everyone into their seats.

It didn't stop their stares and whispered taunts though. By the time the bell went, I was ready to get the hell out of there. But I traded one hell for another, bumping straight into Avery.

"Watch it," he sneered.

"Sorry, I was just—"

"Yeah, whatever." He went to stalk off.

"The pep rally tonight, you'll be there?" The words spilled out in a desperate attempt to make him talk to me.

Of course he would be there... it was a pep rally for *his* team.

He stared at me like I'd grown a second head. "Yeah, I'll be there. Don't tell me you're thinking of coming?" Contempt dripped from his words.

"Yeah, well... for research." I ducked my head, my heart crashing wildly in my chest. His hatred for me bled from him like a river, washing over me until I felt like I couldn't breathe.

"Avery, I am sor—"

"Didn't you screw Chase over enough already, snitch?" The sudden weight of Micah's arm draped over my shoulder made me flinch.

My eyes found Avery's again and the air instantly cooled between us. I braced myself for his retort, but instead he spun on his heel and walked away.

"Shit, snitch, what the fuck did you say?"

"Get the hell off me, Micah." I nudged him away from me and flicked my hair off my shoulder. "You don't have to be such a dick all the time."

"Says the girl who single-handedly screwed us over." He scowled.

"I'm not doing this with you." I dodged around him, but he grabbed my bag strap and yanked me back.

"Not so fast, snitch." I glanced back, arching a brow, refusing to show even an ounce of weakness. "Little word of advice." The corner of his mouth lifted into a vicious smirk. "Stay the fuck away from Avery."

———

UNTIL LAST YEAR when I'd made the cheer squad, I'd never been to the football stadium before. It felt strange coming back here to sit in the bleachers. Kids gave me a wide berth as I tried to find a seat, stepping aside or bunching up to their friends as if they might catch some contagious disease from any contact with me.

It didn't bother me. I hadn't exactly been a social butterfly before the paper ran the exposé. I preferred my own company, reading books and watching real life crime documentaries. I had friends, my co-writers at the paper and my colleagues at the library. I just didn't have *close* friends. Except my mom. She was my best friend. Always had been, always would be.

Eventually, I found a seat on the end of a row. The guy next to me scooched closer to his friends and I shook my head.

"You won't catch anything."

"I don't know, I heard you gave Micah Delfine crabs?"

"What? I didn't—" I rolled my lips together, refusing to feed the rumor mill. Clearly Micah wanted to play dirty.

"He's just covering for the fact that he couldn't last, if you know what I'm saying. All that locker room talk of Micah Delfine going all night long..." I beckoned the guy closer, my lips curving with amusement. "I heard he pays the cheerleaders to spread rumors that he's an energizer bunny in the sack, but he's more of a floppy duck if you catch my drift."

"Oh, shit." The guy exploded with laughter, leaning over to tell his friends.

I smiled, satisfied. But then it quickly died when I realized I'd potentially poked the beast.

CHAPTER FIVE

Avery

THE CROWD ROARED my name as I stepped up beside Coach.

Chase.

Chase.

Chase.

It filled the football field like a battle cry, rippling through me like a wave hurtling toward the shore.

But I knew that come game day, it would be ten times as loud. Because the whole of Rixon would turn out to see our first game of the season.

"Did you tell him yet?" Coach Ford asked me out of the corner of his mouth as we watched the cheer squad do their thing.

"No, but I will."

"You have until Monday. I won't lie to him, Avery. He's my best friend."

"And I'm your star player," I quipped, earning me a nudge to the shoulder.

"Watch it, kid. You might be my star player, but it doesn't mean I'm going to give you an easy time this season." He nodded over to the bleachers. "I see Miss Fuller came."

"Hadn't noticed," I grumbled.

"Of course you hadn't. It might have been light years ago, but I remember what it was like to be seventeen."

"Mom told me you fought your feelings for Felicity for most of senior year."

"Your mom talks too much. But yeah, I was an asshole back then."

"Then? I hate to tell you Coach but you're still kind of an asshole."

His deep laughter reverberated through him, but then the cheer squad made their grand finale, and all eyes were back on the team.

Coach stepped up to the mic and the crowd ushered into silence. Anticipation rippled through the air. "Rixon High," he said, "are you ready to play some football?"

The bleachers exploded, the chorus of hoots and hollers hitting us like a forcefield. The rest of the guys joined in, cheering and clapping, while the team mascot, a huge foam Viking head worked the crowd into even more of a frenzy.

"Okay, okay," Coach boomed. "Last year we got our asses handed to us by Marshall, but this year we're bringing that championship title home. And the guy that's going to get us there... your quarterback and captain, Avery Chase."

It was a heavy burden to carry, the hopes and dreams of every teacher, every single kid at Rixon High, their parents, my teammates. But I bore it with pride and honor. As I stepped up to the mic, a sense of deep responsibility weighed down on me. But nothing worth having came easy. You had to fight for it tooth and nail. You had to dig your heels in and keep going. If my dad and Coach Ford had taught me anything, it was that it wasn't about being the best, it was about being better than you were yesterday.

Last season, we'd lost. We'd let the championship slip between our fingers. But this season, it was not an option.

I needed to go out on a high, to leave my mark, and follow in my dad's footsteps.

So I would push. I would push my team and myself and our fans...

And I would win.

———

I FOLLOWED the guys out of the locker room to the stadium parking lot. We were heading to Micah's house for the after-party. His parents were out of town a lot and his older brother worked shifts, so he was home alone most weekends, which made his house the preferred hangout for the team.

"Yo, Chase, look who I found sneaking around."

I ground to a halt, dread flooding my chest as I watched Micah steer Miley toward me. He had his arm roped around her neck like she was one of the guys.

"Snitch wants to party with us."

"I never said that," she snapped, elbowing him in the ribs. Micah yelped as she ducked out from under his arm.

"No, but you were hovering around waiting for us to leave..." He rubbed his jaw, assessing her with his dark eyes. "So I got to wonder if you were hoping for an invitation or whether you planned to follow us like the creep you are."

"Go to hell," she sneered.

"What, scared, snitch?"

"I've been to your parties before and they suck."

Surprise registered on Micah's face. "Well you weren't doing it right." He stepped up to her, and my spine went rigid. "Because my parties are fucking epic."

Micah wasn't a bad guy; he just didn't know when to quit. He loved the fan worship, the way girls went ga-ga over football players. He lapped up the attention and power. A lot of the guys did, and I didn't blame them. It was something to be so young and be so revered and adored. In the eyes of Rixon, we could do no wrong.

Like tonight. No one would bat an eyelid at the party out at the Delfine's house. So long as we kept it under control, parents, the adults, even the local police were happy to let us do our thing because we were Raiders. And wearing that jersey meant something.

"Look at her, man. She doesn't want to come to the party. She looks like a rabbit caught in the headlights," I said, refusing to look at her.

"I think she does," he countered.

"Micah," an exasperated breath left my lips, "just leave—"

"I'll come."

My head whipped around to meet Miley's narrowed gaze. "Excuse me?"

"You heard me."

"Fuck, yes. You and me, snitch. It's going down. I hope you can hold your liquor."

"One, there is no 'you and me,' and two, I said I'll come to the party, not that I'll get drunk."

Micah slung his arm around her shoulder again and smirked. "We'll see. Let's go."

My brows bunched together as I watched him guide her toward his car wondering what the fuck was happening right now.

I didn't want her at the party. I didn't want her anywhere near me. But Miley climbed into his car, glancing over at me at the last second. She didn't look confused or even scared... she looked determined.

She looked like she was a girl on a mission. But she'd been that girl before, and it hadn't ended well for anyone.

Especially me.

———

BY THE TIME I arrived at the party, Micah already had Miley drinking one of his concoctions.

"What's going on?" I hissed, while she chatted to Ben and Petey.

"What? Just giving her a little behind the scenes access." He grinned, letting his eyes flick back over to her. "She's pretty hot for a nerd."

"This is a bad idea," I said.

"Because you're pissed at her still, or because you have a thing for the snitch?"

"What the fuck, man?" I balked.

"Oh, come on. You think I haven't noticed the giant stick up your ass ever since last spring? Did something happen between the two of you?"

"Nothing happened. And don't go spreading that shit around. She screwed me over just as much as the rest of you, that's all. I don't want her here because she doesn't fucking belong here."

A trickle of awareness ran up my spine and Micah's gaze went over my shoulder.

Shit.

She was behind me, listening to every word. When I turned slightly to meet her dejected expression, my blood turned to ice. How was it possible I felt so much for a girl I hardly knew? But I'd been getting to know her.

It was months ago. The article hadn't run

until right before school broke for the summer, but Miley had quit the cheer team long before that.

"I think I'll have another." Miley waved her empty cup at Micah and he whooped.

"My kind of girl."

Grabbing her wrist, I yanked her out of the kitchen and down the quiet, darkened hall. The majority of kids were outside, enjoying the lingering warmth of summer.

"What the hell, Avery?" Miley hissed, snatching her hand back.

"What the fuck are you doing?"

"I was enjoying myself until you rudely interrupted me."

"What game are you playing?" I studied her face. Heart-shaped pouty lips, a button nose littered with freckles, and tawny eyes that looked right through me. She was pretty, gorgeous even, but I knew it was a smokescreen for the treacherous snake she really was.

"I was invited."

"But why? Why the hell would you want to come here and be at a party no one wants you at?"

"Micah wants me—"

"Micah wants to get you drunk and then

embarrass you." Anger rolled through me, but it wasn't only at her, it was at what she'd said.

Micah wants me.

He didn't, I knew that. But I wouldn't put it past him to try something with her just to spread a vicious rumor Monday at school.

I released a frustrated breath. "You should go before you make things any worse for yourself."

There was that dejected look again. What right did she have feeling hurt, when she'd completely betrayed me and the team?

"You hate me, I get it. I do." She took a shuddering breath. "But I still need to write this article, and I don't quit. Ever."

"Well, maybe you should." I glowered at her, the air crackling between us.

Just then, a couple of guys stumbled down the hall, knocking me straight into Miley. My hands automatically went to her shoulders, steadying her as we careened into the wall.

"Thanks," she croaked, her eyes darting to my mouth. My dick twitched, more than ready to roll with whatever was happening between us. I moved closer, pressing the lines of my body against hers. Miley's breath caught, her lips parting on a soft gasp.

"Avery?" she said, my name a rough whisper.

My heart crashed against my chest, my palms slick and hands shaking. My body remembered; the fickle fucking thing remembered what it was like to have her so close. Close enough to kiss... to taste.

"Avery?" she said again, leaning in enough that I felt her warm liquor-scented breath.

I didn't want to kiss her.

I didn't want to even *think* about kissing her.

But I couldn't stop myself. She pulled me in like gravity until my lips ghosted over hers in a featherlight touch that made her shiver.

"Miley," her name formed on my tongue but then music boomed through the house, ripping me from the moment. I staggered back, blinking at her. A crestfallen expression washed over her.

"You need to go," I barked, before taking off down the hall.

"Where'd you go?" Micah smirked as I headed straight for the cooler and grabbed a beer.

"To tell her to get the hell out of here, why?"

"No reason." His eyes danced with amusement, but I didn't stick around for any more of his interrogations. I slipped outside into his massive yard and found a quiet spot over by the firepit.

It wasn't long before a girl sought me out.

"Hey, Avery. Why are you sitting out here all

alone?" Kendall Novak lowered herself into my lap as if she owned me. Sliding her arms around my neck, she leaned forward a little, giving me a front row ticket to her impressive cleavage.

Kendall was a cheerleader. She wasn't captain, but everyone knew she was the favorite. And she'd had her eye on me since I'd become first string quarterback in sophomore year. But I didn't date. And I especially didn't date girls like Kendall. They were too clingy, too high maintenance, and once they got their claws into you, they became a bad rash you couldn't shake. I didn't have the time or energy for that.

But that didn't mean my dick didn't want a taste. She was hot as fuck and I was as horny as the next guy.

"Avery?" she purred, commanding my attention.

"Just chilling," I said, aware of her tight little body pressed up against mine in all the right places. If she wiggled her ass, she'd be as good as grinding on my dick.

Laughter filled the air as Micah and the rest of the guys spilled outside, Miley still tucked under his arm.

"Seriously, what's with Micah and the snitch?"

"Beats me," I ground out. She still looked like a rabbit caught in headlights.

Why the fuck was she still here?

As if she heard me, her eyes snapped over in my direction, widening when she saw Kendall. Without thinking, I slipped my arm around her waist and brought my lips to her neck, not taking my eyes off of Miley as I kissed her soft skin.

Even though she was across the yard, I saw the hitch in her breath. Hurt flashed over her face, and for a second, I felt triumphant. Until she took off toward the pool with Micah.

What the fuck was he doing?

And more importantly, what the fuck was she doing?

CHAPTER SIX

Miley

I'D MADE A MISTAKE.

When Avery had made it obvious he didn't want me at the party, I'd dug in my heels and accepted Micah's invitation. But now I was watching Avery cuddle up to Kendall Novak while I pretended I could party like one of them—the cool kids, the popular kids, the kids I'd spent my entire life avoiding— all while trying to keep control of my reflexes.

I felt a little weird though. I'd only had like one or two drinks when we first arrived, and Micah had given them to me directly. And I'd eaten a handful of the snacks out on the counter while I stood around listening to them talk about the upcoming season. So it wasn't like I'd been drinking on an empty stomach.

"It's warm out here," I said, tugging on Micah's hand. I knew he was probably setting me up for some big fall, but I couldn't back down. Not now.

"You should lose the cardigan," he suggested.

"Good idea." I pulled it off my arms and draped it over the back of a garden lounger. Kids were littered around the yard, huddled in groups chatting and dancing, while others played water polo in the pool.

The water looked so inviting, rippling and shimmering under the moonlight.

"Better?" Micah brushed his finger over my shoulder and a shiver rolled through me. His touch was nice, comforting. But he was supposed to be the bad guy, wasn't he?

Avery was the good guy. He was the leader; the cool, composed captain. Only, when I glanced over at him, he was practically making out with Kendall.

My stomach dropped.

He was kissing her...

I didn't come here so he could kiss her, I came here so he would kiss me.

"Hey, Miley, come meet some people." Micah

beckoned me over and I stuffed down all my thoughts about Avery.

"Hey." I smiled, my cheeks aching.

"You know Christina and Thea. That's Jordan, Kercher, and Sam."

I lifted my hand in a small wave. "Hey."

"Didn't think we'd see you around here again." Christina glowered at me.

"We all deserve a second chance, right?" I exploded with laughter, the five of them staring at me with a mix of confusion and amusement.

"You should take it easy, babe," Micah whispered.

A song blasted out over the sound system and I did a little leap on the spot. "I love this one." My hips began to move as I felt my limbs follow. I didn't usually dance, but I couldn't seem to stand still. Beads of sweat trickled down my back and between my cleavage as I stood on the edge of the pool, dancing in my own little world.

"Micah, come join me," I hollered.

"Oh, I'm good," he smirked, "just enjoying the view."

I shrugged, letting the music carry me away to another place. I hadn't felt so free in a long time. My body felt relaxed and my thoughts were mellow.

Whatever beer they were serving here was good stuff because I felt freaking great.

"You look a little hot, Miley. You should take your t-shirt off."

"You think?" My brows knitted. It made my face feel weird and I touched a finger to my cheeks.

"Yeah, babe. All the girls are in bikini tops, look." He nodded over to the pool, and sure enough, most of the girls sitting around the edge were half-naked.

"It'll be fine, babe." Micah gave me a reassuring smile, and before I knew it, I was pulling off my t-shirt. The crowd cheered, and I blushed from head to toe, but I was so warm, and I didn't want to end up a sweaty mess before the night was out.

The balmy air felt great on my heated skin and I balled up my t-shirt and threw it at Micah.

"Hell, yeah," he wolf-whistled, setting off the crowd again. I didn't know what they were cheering and laughing at. But I didn't care. Everything felt too good. I felt too good.

"What the fuck?" A voice boomed, and I looked around to find Avery marching toward us.

He looked pissed; his sexy jaw clenched tight as his eyes lasered in on Micah. "What the fuck are you doing?"

"She was a little hot." Micah shrugged.

"Put your t-shirt back on." Avery snatched it off his friend and held it out for me.

"But all the girls are—"

"Just put it on, Miley."

"Relax, man, we were just having a little fun. Weren't we, snitch?"

My chest tightened.

Snitch.

That's what they all called me before...

"You called me snitch," I said, planting my hands on my hips. "That's not a very nice thing to call your friend and I thought we were friends now."

"Nah, baby, we were never friends. Just thought you should get a little taste of your own medicine."

My eyes narrowed. His face looked funny. Everything looked a little funny. Faces were elongated and wobbly, the trees growing into huge giants in the distance. I blinked rapidly, trying to make it all go away.

"I don't feel so good."

"What the fuck did you give her?"

"Just a few edibles..."

"You're a real fucking idiot at times."

Avery wrapped his arm around my side, steadying me. But I felt sick all of a sudden, like I was spinning on the Tilt-A-Whirl at the funfair.

"I don't feel so good," I repeated.

"Come on," he said, "let's get you out of here."

"Chase, come on, man, it was a joke."

"Fucking asshole."

I slumped against Avery's side, my stomach churning.

"Think you can make it to my car?" was the last thing I heard before I leaned over and puked all over myself.

———

THE RIDE back to my house was quiet. After I'd puked up the entire contents of my stomach, Avery found me a bottle of water and some paper towels and I'd managed to clean myself up enough to go home.

I felt like shit. My head and tummy hurt so bad, but Avery assured me it would wear off by morning.

"How are you holding up over there?"

"I'll live." I couldn't look at him. He'd seen me like that, high as a kite dancing in my bra to an audience who were laughing at me.

God, I was an idiot.

"You shouldn't have come tonight."

"You think I don't know that?" I hissed.

"So, why did you?"

"I don't know." My shoulders lifted in a small shrug as I peeked over at him. He looked so freaking good in his Raiders jersey and ball cap pulled on backwards. And I was a mess.

"I think you do."

"Fine. You want to know the truth? I came because I know I screwed up. I get it, okay? I thought if you'd just give me a chance to explain, that maybe we could—"

"There is no 'we,' Miley." He rolled up outside my house and cut the engine. "You need to get that into your head. Anything that happened between us in junior year was a mistake."

I knew I'd hurt Avery, betrayed his confidence, so I guess I should have been prepared for his cruel words, but I couldn't process what he was saying. Because I still felt it. I still felt the tether between us every time he was near.

And he... didn't?

"You don't mean that," I whispered, the words thick in my throat.

"Yeah," he let out a steady breath, "I do. You lied to me for months, let me think you were someone else. That you were this smart, funny, cool girl determined to push her boundaries and try new things. I fell for you, Miley, and you fucking betrayed me."

"You fell for me?" Hope blossomed in my chest.

"No, I fell for that girl. The one you pretended to be. I didn't fall for you."

"Oh." God, it hurt.

It hurt so freaking much.

I'd spent all summer trying to figure out a way to make it up to Avery. I'd written list after list, plotted all the ways I'd make him see that what we'd shared was real.

But it didn't matter. I realized that now.

He didn't want me. He never had. He'd wanted the girl I'd become undercover. The quietly confident cheerleader out to make the most of her junior year.

I'd surprised everyone at tryouts last year. Half the girls didn't even recognize me, someone they'd gone to school with for the last two years. But that only aided my cause. No one had paid me any attention previously, so I could carve out my own story. Get close to them and become their new interesting friend.

And it had worked.

But I hadn't banked on getting close to the star quarterback. It had happened by accident. I'd been early for practice one day and he'd been running drills with Coach on the football field. I heard him telling Coach he was struggling in English class and I offered to tutor him.

Avery didn't want anyone to know, so for almost six months, we'd studied in private. It was the perfect ruse at first, a chance to really get to know Rixon's golden boy. By the time spring rolled around, and the article was due, I'd slowly started making excuses to miss our appointments.

Then one day, he'd kissed me.

Avery Chase kissed me.

I'd been so shocked, so confused... that I'd sat there dumbfounded.

I'd never returned his calls after that. Because the truth was, I'd fallen for him. I'd fallen for my mark. And it was so cliché, so ridiculous, that I tried to pretend it had never happened.

Until the final newspaper hit the halls at school.

God, I still remembered seeing Avery right after it went live. The anger in his eyes. The bitter disappointment. It was the talk of the school.

I was the talk of the school.

And Avery had looked at me with complete disgust.

"Look, something tells me Coach isn't going to

let either of us wiggle our way out of this, so let's just call a truce. I'll keep the guys in line, if you promise no more theatrics."

"I can do that."

I needed to get out of his car. The air was too thick, and I felt nauseous again.

"Are you okay, you look a little green again?"

"I'm fine," I rushed out, grabbing the door handle. "And thank you for tonight. It won't happen again. From now on, I'll be nothing but professional."

"Glad to hear it."

"Well, I guess I'll see you around then."

"Yeah." An awkward silence followed and I couldn't take it for a second longer, so I shouldered the door and stumbled out...

Dragging my withering heart with me.

———

I KEPT my distance after that.

Monday at school after my edible-induced show was interesting. I'd entered the building to a loud applause and hollers of 'strip for me, snitch.'

But once the laughter subsided, Avery, true to his word, kept the team off my back. I observed their practices and interviewed a couple of the new players about their experiences so far. Coach gave me a ton of game footage to watch and made his staff available for interviews. Avery avoided me like the plague, and I did the same with him.

After his confession, my heart felt more bruised than ever.

"How's the article coming?" Mr. Jones asked me as he entered the Rixon Riot HQ on Thursday afternoon. I was finishing up my day's notes.

"It's... coming. Give it a couple more weeks and I'll have plenty to work with." I shoved everything in my bag.

"That's what I want to hear. If we want to run a Homecoming edition, I'm going to need your final draft in two weeks."

"You got it, sir."

Ugh. Homecoming. The social event of the year that celebrated both football and school spirit.

At least the article would be finished by then, so I wouldn't have to go in the name of reporting.

"Now go on, get out of here. You must have more exciting things to do on a Thursday afternoon than hang out here." He smiled.

"Yeah, exciting things."

He obviously hadn't heard the rumors about all my excitement at the party. But that was the thing with kids, they were good at hiding things. Rumors, fights, parties... there was some unspoken word that what happened between teenagers stayed between teenagers.

I shouldered the door and slipped into the hall. School was already half empty. I'd almost reached the main doors when I heard a shriek from the girl's bathroom.

Without thinking, I ran inside.

"Lily?" I said, eyes wide with horror as I watched the gang of girls slowly back away from her.

"What did you do to her?" I snapped.

"N-nothing," one of them said. "We were just... talking, and she started pulling her hair and screaming at us."

"Did they hurt you?" It came out softer as I met Lily's frantic gaze. She shook her head, but I didn't like the fear in her eyes.

"You," I jabbed my finger at the ringleader. "What's your name?"

"Why do I need to tell you?"

I grabbed the collar of her blouse. "I said, *name*."

"L-Lindsey Filmer."

"If she's hurt, I will make sure Principal Kiln knows about this."

"We were just messing around. It wasn't—"

Lily started sobbing again and I moved closer, putting myself between her and the girls.

"Get out of here, all of you."

They scurried out, leaving the bathroom in thick silence. Lily's face was lowered as she pulled furiously at her hair.

I crouched down and laid my hands gently on hers. "Lily," I said softly. "Look at me."

Slowly, she lifted her eyes to mine.

"They're gone, see. It's just you and me."

"T-they're gone?"

"Yes. Now do you want to tell me what happened?"

"I..." She hesitated and I gave her a reassuring smile.

"It's okay. You don't have to tell me anything. Is there someone I can call? Ashleigh?"

I'd seen her hanging out with Avery's sister.

"She got picked up early for a dental appointment."

"Your mom?"

Lily dragged her bottom lip between her teeth, giving me a little shake of her head.

"Avery is at practice. I could sit with you until they get done?"

"Okay."

I stood up and offered her my hand. Lily accepted it, letting me pull her up. She seemed better now, calmer. But she'd been so afraid when I first got here, cowering against the wall, trying to disappear. I knew girls could be cruel, but something told me there was more to the story than she was willing to offer.

CHAPTER SEVEN

Avery

WE WERE LISTENING to Coach tear us a new one about our sloppy performance when I noticed Miley and Lily over by the bleachers. Something wasn't right. For two girls who, to my best knowledge didn't know one another, they were standing a little too closely. Lily glanced toward us and shook her head, before darting out of eyesight.

Strange.

"Okay, hit the showers," Coach said. But I didn't head for the locker room, jogging over to Miley instead.

"What happened?" I said.

"There was an incident."

"Incident, what kind of incident?" I craned my neck around Miley to try to see Lily, but she was hiding in the shadows.

"What the fuck happened?" It came out harsher than I intended, guilt stabbing at my chest. But after almost a week of avoiding Miley, I hadn't anticipated on seeing her.

"I found her in the girl's bathroom. She was crying, pulling her hair... There was a group of girls. I don't think they hurt—"

"Fuck." I ran a hand over my jaw. "I should get her dad—"

"No. She freaked out on the way here. Said she didn't want him to find out. But I didn't know what else to do."

"You did the right thing. Can you stay with her until I've grabbed my things? I'll be like ten minutes, fifteen at the most." I glanced over my shoulder. Coach was nowhere to be seen, but I didn't want to lie to his face. So I had to hope he was already holed up in his office.

"Of course." She smiled.

Miley smiled and it was like a punch to the gut.

"Tell Lily I'll be as quick as I can and that we'll figure it out, okay?"

"What happened to her?"

"It's a long story. But thanks... for doing this."

She nodded, her eyes glittering with indecipherable emotion.

"Meet me in the parking lot in fifteen minutes."

"Okay." Miley watched me leave. I didn't want to. I wanted to go to Lily and find out what the hell had happened, but I respected her wishes not to have her dad find out just yet. That wouldn't end well for anyone.

I jogged back across the field and went into the locker room. Thankfully, there was no sign of Coach.

"Saw you talking to the snitch," Micah said. "What did she want?"

"Leave it." I gave him a hard look and went to move around him to my locker cage, but he pressed his hand against my chest.

"Come on, man. I know you're not still pissed about the party. It was a joke."

"You knowingly gave her edibles. Not cool, asshole. Imagine if some douchebag had done that to your sister."

"But she's not... your sister."

"Whatever, Micah. I need to get my stuff." I barged past him and quickly changed into my clothes. A shower would have to wait.

"In a hurry, Chase?" One of the guys chuckled.

"Gotta take care of some family stuff."

Because although Lily wasn't my sister, she was family. And after everything she'd been through, she needed me.

————

MILEY AND LILY were waiting at my car.

"Did you see my dad?" she rushed out.

"Relax, Lil, he was holed up in his office."

"Good, that's good."

But from the way she was pulling at her hair, I knew it wasn't good.

"I'm going to give you a ride home and—"

"N-no, not yet. I'll be okay, I just need some time to calm down."

"So where do you want to go? Ashleigh won't be home for a little while."

"Ice cream. I could eat ice cream."

"Fine, we can stop by Ice T's."

"I'll just—" Miley thumbed to nowhere in particular. "Bye, Lily." She gave her a small wave.

"You're not coming?" Lily's eyes widened.

Fuck.

I internally groaned. This could not be happening.

"Well, no, I wasn't going to... I mean, I'm not sure Avery wants me there."

"What? Why not?"

"It's fine," I grumbled. "You can come."

"Are you sure? I don't want to—"

"Please," Lily added. "I like you. You don't ask too many questions and you're kind."

"I guess I could eat some ice cream."

"Thank you," Lily dragged her to the backseat and the two of them climbed in while I went around the driver's side.

Not how I imagined spending the night before my first game of the season, but it was Lily. I couldn't just abandon her.

It took us less than ten minutes to get to Ice T's and find a parking spot. The girls had been quiet on the ride here, so it was a relief to climb out of the car and inhale some fresh air.

"Mint chocolate chip, Lil?" I asked her as we approached the door.

"With sprinkles."

"With sprinkles." I chuckled. She'd eaten the same flavor ice cream for as long as I could remember. Our dads used to bring us here all the time when we were kids. We'd take over the small store: me and Ashleigh, Lily and Poppy, and the Bennet twins and Ezra.

I grabbed the door and she disappeared inside. My eyes slid to Miley's and her cheeks pinked.

"Oh, after you," she said.

"I got it." I motioned for her to go on in and she slipped past me, her body brushing mine.

Fuck. Her touch, no matter how light, did things to me. Things I didn't want to feel.

I told the girls to grab a seat and joined the line, bracing myself for the onslaught of comments.

"Hey, Avery, looking good this season."

"Are you going to bring home that championship?"

"Go Raiders."

It wasn't anything I hadn't heard a hundred times already, but it felt different with Miley here, watching me interact with fans.

Two kids asked their mom to take a photo with me and I crouched down, hugging them to my side.

"Say cheese," I said, and one of them snorted.

"Don't you mean say, 'Go Raiders?'"

"Okay, whatever you want buddy. On three. One... two..."

They shrieked 'Go Raiders' at the top of their lungs, making the entire store laugh.

"Thank you," the mom said. "You're their idol."

"Thank you, ma'am."

Thankfully, I was up next, and the server was super quick at dishing up our order.

"That was sweet," Miley said when I reached the table. "Does it happen a lot?"

"Not—"

"All the time," Lily piped up, digging her spoon into the pale-green ice cream. "He's basically a celebrity."

"Lil." I rolled my eyes.

"I'm pretty sure I saw those girls back there sneak a photo of you when you weren't looking." Miley's brow arched with amusement.

"It happens." I shrugged, digging into my own ice cream.

"So, are you two friends?" Lily asked, and I almost choked on my caramel swirl.

"We... uh, it's complicated." Miley ducked her head, but I caught the flash of guilt in her eyes.

"Oooh, have you hooked up?"

"Lily!" My eyes grew to saucers.

"What?" Her shoulders lifted. "It's just a question and you're all weird around each other. Ashleigh said you've never had a girlfriend before. Do you want Miley to be your girlfriend?"

"Jesus," I mumbled under my breath. Miley smothered the soft laughter bubbling in her chest.

"I'm glad you're feeling a bit better," she said to Lily. The way she handled Coach's daughter, with patience and compassion, was impressive.

Lily was an awkward kid; she always had been. If she knew you, she could talk your ear off, but if you were meeting her for the first time, chances were she wouldn't make a sound.

But not with Miley though. She liked Miley.

"Do you want to tell me what happened?" I said, hoping to God I wouldn't have to go to Coach.

"It was nothing really." Lily's eyes darted to her bowl as she swirled the spoon through her melting ice cream.

"Lil, I can't help if you don't tell me what happened."

"Some girls cornered me in the girl's bathroom. They didn't do anything... they were just asking me all these questions. About dad... about you... about the team. But they surrounded me, and I couldn't think. And they kept asking and asking... and it got louder, and my heart started beating harder—"

"Hey," Miley laid her hand over Lily's. "It's okay. You're okay now."

"T-thanks."

"Who were these girls?"

"Oh no, I don't want to get anyone into trouble." Her eyes flicked to Miley, fear glittering there.

"Lil, if someone is upsetting you, we need to tell your dad—"

"No! He'll go to Principal Kiln and then I'll be a snitch and it'll make everything worse."

Miley flinched. "I'm going to the restroom. I'll be right back." She hurried away and Lily frowned.

"Is she okay?"

"Yeah, she's fine. I'm more worried about you. How about I make you a deal? You promise to talk to Mrs. Bennet, and I won't tell your dad."

"I don't know... won't she have to tell him?"

"She's the guidance counsellor, Lil. She's there to help you. And if you ask her not to tell your dad, she won't."

"I'll think about it."

"Good. And if you change your mind and want to tell me who it was, I'll talk to them. They'll listen to me."

"Oh my God, your head just grew like three sizes." She pinched my arm and I exploded with laughter.

"Thanks," she said, giving me a weak smile. "For doing this."

"Anytime, Lil. You know that."

Miley slid into her chair. "Everything good?"

"Yeah," I said, feeling the lingering tension between us return.

But it only amplified when Lily glanced at Miley and said, "Do you want to come to the game with me tomorrow?"

"Oh, I can't, I didn't get a ticket."

"My dad is the coach, I'm sure he can get you one."

"Lil," I warned. She was trying to play Cupid, and it would have been cute, if it wasn't for the fact that every time I thought about kissing Miley—and I'd thought about it a lot since we got to Ice T's—I remembered her betrayal.

"I appreciate the offer, but I can't make it. Not tomorrow."

"Maybe another time then?"

"Yeah, maybe." Miley caught my eye, but quickly glanced away.

"Ready to go home?"

"Yeah, I guess."

"Come on then."

We made our way back to my car, but Miley hesitated. "I can walk."

"No way. Avery can take me home first and then take you, can't you?"

"It's fine. I'll just wal—"

"Get in the car," I sighed.

"I don't want to be a nuisance."

"Miley, just get in the damn car." I yelled, yanking the door open. She slipped inside. When Lily went to pass me, I pinned her with a hard look. "You need to stop."

"I'm not doing anything." She smirked.

"You know exactly what you're doing, and it's not cool."

"I have no idea what you're talking about." Like hell she didn't.

Lily ducked inside the car and I slammed her door behind her, wondering how I could dominate the football field and come up against some of the biggest defensive players in the country, and be schooled by a ninth grader.

CHAPTER EIGHT

Miley

"SHE'S A SWEET KID," I said, watching Lily take off toward her house. She paused at the porch and glanced back, waving at us.

"She's a pain in my ass," Avery grunted. "Same with my sister. The two of them together... that's when you really need to be worried."

We shared a quiet laugh. I'd spent months watching Avery from afar, then tutoring him. But he'd always been like a closed book. I hadn't *seen* him. The guy underneath the shoulder pads and helmet.

Not until it was too late.

"She was really scared when I found her," I said.

"You know the girls who did it?"

"I got one of their names, yeah."

"Good," he said. "I'm going to need you to tell it to me."

"Avery, Lily said—"

"I know what she said, Miley, but she's just a kid. And these girls, they think just because she's Jason Ford's daughter they can use her, or pick on her, or climb over her to get to him."

"And you?" I asked.

"Yeah, and me. It's whack, I know. But you've got to understand something about this town, football is the life force that drives everything."

"You think I don't know that?" It was one of the reasons I'd written the exposé. The PTA, teachers, Principal Kiln, even the local police department, they were all blinded to the team's thrall. The Rixon Raiders football players could do no wrong in their eyes, while the rest of us mere mortals sat by and watched.

It wasn't fair. At least, it hadn't felt fair last year when I'd become one of them. An insider. Being a cheerleader gave you a certain amount of social status. It wasn't the same as being a football player, but it had given me a front row seat.

Now... now I didn't know what to think. The

guys worked hard on the field, really freaking hard, and for some of the players, football was their only shot at college. Because without an athletic scholarship, they had nothing. But it still didn't excuse putting the team on a pedestal and letting them bend the rules the rest of us had to follow.

He released a steady breath. "Forget I said anything."

The silence was awkward. Thick and suffocating. I knew he hated me, hated everything that I was, everything I stood for. But he didn't know how much I regretted what went down between us, because he hadn't given me the chance to explain.

Tell him while he can't escape.

I smoothed my hands over my thighs, trying to pluck up the courage. It wasn't like he could go anywhere, and part of me knew if I didn't tell him now, I might never get the chance.

"You know how football means everything to you..."

"Yeah?"

"Well, writing means everything to me. I've had my heart set on going to Northwestern since I can remember."

"I don't understand what this has to do with me." His eyes slid to mine, confusion furrowing his brows.

"I'm just saying... you'd do anything to win, right? Anything to make sure the team comes out on top? Well, I'd do anything to... to make sure I come out on top, I mean."

He let out a frustrated sigh. "It's not the same thing, Miley."

"I'm sorry."

"Yeah, me too."

We didn't talk again. Avery was lost in his own thoughts, and I was too busy wishing the seat would gobble me up.

I'd blown it.

Any chance I'd had with Avery had gone up in flames when the exposé had gone live. I'd chosen my future over everything else.

What was that saying though? You didn't know what you'd lost until it was gone?

I was beginning to think there was some merit in that.

He finally pulled up outside my house.

"Well, this is me," I said.

He pursed his lips.

"I'll guess I'll just..." I thumbed to my house. "Good luck at the game tomorrow."

"Thanks."

"I'll be seeing you then."

"Okay."

"Okay."

The air crackled between us. His eyes homed in on my lips again and I wondered what it would be like to kiss him. Would he push me away or pull me closer?

"At least there isn't long before I have to submit my article." I laughed, but it came out strangled. "Then you'll never have to see me again."

His eyes shuttered.

"Avery?" I croaked.

But then he was on me, his hands buried deep in my hair, kissing me. My hands twisted into his jersey, pulling him closer, fireworks going off inside my stomach.

Avery was kissing me.

And it was everything.

His tongue curled around mine as his lips devoured me. He tasted so yummy, like caramel and chocolate. I never wanted to come up for air.

Slowly, he pulled away, touching his head to mine as we both caught our breath.

"That was amazing." I smiled so wide my cheeks hurt. Feeling confident, I leaned in and brushed my lips over his again.

But he didn't kiss me back.

My stomach plummeted into my toes. Not again. He wouldn't do that...

"Avery?" My voice cracked. I felt his breath warm on my face, the sickly-sweet scent on his lips.

"You should go."

I jerked back as if he'd slapped me. "But I thought—"

"You thought wrong." His expression hardened. "This was a—"

"Mistake. Yeah, I got the memo the first time. You know?" I sucked in a sharp breath, trying to swallow the tears rushing up my throat, "I know I did a really shitty thing to you, Avery. And if I could, I would take it back..."

He stared blankly at me, and I knew I'd lost him. He hated me too much to let the past go.

"You're right, this was a mistake." I shouldered the car door and scrambled out.

"Miley, wait..." Avery called after me, but I didn't look back. I couldn't. He'd trampled on my heart again, and although I knew it was only what I deserved, it didn't stop the tears from falling.

———

THE RAIDERS WON. It was the only thing anyone was talking about Monday morning at school. I walked the halls invisible, as kids still rode the high of the win.

"Miley," a voice called, and I glanced over my shoulder to find Lily and Ashleigh approaching me.

"Hey, Lily. How are you?"

"I'm okay, thanks." She smiled. "I missed you at the game Friday. Avery scored two touchdowns. He was amazing."

"Gross, Lil, that's my brother you're talking about." Ashleigh chuckled. "I'm Ashleigh," she said. "You must be Miley. Lily told me all about you."

"She did, huh? All good things, I hope."

"She said you and my brother had some crazy chemistry at Ice T's."

"I... really don't know what to say to that." I flushed.

"My brother's never had a girlfriend before."

"Oh, I'm not his—"

"I know." She snickered. "But you could be."

The thought made my stomach clench. But it was a fantasy. Avery didn't want to talk to me, let alone be with me.

"Oh, I don't know about that. Your brother isn't exactly my number one fan."

"Because of the article you wrote about the team?"

"I see you've done your research," I said.

"I like to know things. But you helped Lily and I think everyone deserves a second chance, so as long as you don't plan on screwing my brother over again, I think we can be friends." Ashleigh thrust out her hand.

This was so not how I saw my morning going, but I slid my palm against hers and said, "To new friends."

Just then, an announcement came over the speaker that Homecoming tickets were on sale. The hall exploded into cheers, but I wasn't celebrating.

"I can't wait until we're old enough for Homecoming," Ashleigh let out a dreamy sigh.

"Oh, you can go to Homecoming. Anyone can," I corrected her.

"Yeah, I know, but I mean like go... with a guy. No way my dad will let me go on a date yet."

"I bet he'd let you go with Ezra."

"Who's Ezra?"

"He's in our class. Ashleigh has a crush on him." Lily grinned.

"I do not. He's... not my type."

"And what type would that be?" My brow arched.

"Ezra is complicated. We hang out sometimes, but he tends to do his own thing. Hey, we should totally go together." Her face lit up.

"Oh, I don't think so. I'm not a fan of organized social events."

"Please, it'll be fun." Lily gave me a reassuring nod. It was nice to see her more confident than she had been the other day.

"I'm not sure Avery will want me there." And he'd no doubt be crowned Homecoming King.

"Who cares what Avery thinks? He won't want us there either, but that's not going to stop us."

"I'll think about it."

"Excellent." Ashleigh clapped. "We should probably get to class." She grabbed Lily's hand and started pulling her away. "But it was nice to meet you, Miley, and don't let my brother be an ass."

"Oh look, if it isn't the snitch bitch."

I turned around to find Kendall Novak glaring at me.

"Oh, hey, Kendall."

"Why were you talking to Avery's sister just now?"

"That's none of your business."

"It's so sad, using his sister to get to him. When everyone knows Avery wouldn't touch you if you were the last girl on the planet. He told me that much on Saturday night when we were... well, you know." Her lip curved triumphantly as if she could see the daggers wedged in my heart.

"You and Avery—"

"I've waited a long time to call him mine. And I'm not going to stand by and let the likes of some nerd like you get in my way." Kendall leaned in, her saccharine smile vicious. "Stay away from the team and stay away from Avery. Got it?"

"Kendall?" Her name echoed through my skull and we both looked up to find Avery glaring at us.

"Oh. Hey, Avery," she sang, shouldering past me and going to him. She laced her arm through his and they walked off together.

I slumped against my locker bank, inhaling a ragged breath. He'd kissed me and then hooked up with Kendall.

I didn't know why I'd expected anything else. He was Avery Chase. He could have any girl in the school.

Any girl except me.

TUESDAY NIGHT, I was working the late shift at the library. There was only me and old Mrs. Winkleman, and she tended to hang out in her office, listening to classical music and doing the paperwork.

The last person I expected to see come through the door was Avery.

"This is a surprise," I said, smothering my hurt.

"Yeah, well, the school library's Xerox was down, and I need to copy these."

"Sure, I can help you with that. Right this way." I smiled, but he didn't return it.

The Xerox machine was located at the back of the building in an alcove housing the printers and a couple of old computers.

"It's quiet," Avery said.

"We get the odd person who stop by, but usually after seven it's just me and the Winkleman."

"The what?"

"Mrs. Winkleman," I glanced back at him, "she manages the library."

His eyes were dark tonight, brimming with an indecipherable emotion.

"How's Kendall?" I asked, trying to keep my voice even.

"Kendall?" Avery frowned.

"Yeah, I thought... she said you two... it doesn't

matter. It's none of my business." I fumbled with the machine, running my finger over the power switch. Then I ran my staff card through the magnetic strip.

"Okay, she's all set." I refused to look at him. "When you're done, just come back to the desk and pay."

I went to leave, but Avery's hand shot out and snagged my wrist. "Wait," he said.

My eyes finally lifted to his and what I saw there sent a shiver racing down my spine.

"Avery?" I whispered as time stood still.

His eyes were fixated on my mouth, and I swallowed hard, my throat suddenly dry.

"What are you—"

"Shh," he breathed. "Just give me a minute."

"Okay." I nodded.

I'd give him time.

I'd give him all the time in the world.

CHAPTER NINE

Avery

I WANTED TO KISS HER.

Fuck, I wanted to kiss her so badly.

It was like pushing Miley away only made me want her more. It wasn't supposed to be that way. I was supposed to hate her; part of me did. But I couldn't get her out of my head. How cute and goofy she'd looked that night at Micah's party. The way she'd stood up for Lily.

More and more I was beginning to realize Miley Fuller wasn't a bad person. Sure, she'd made some really fucking awful choices, but she was only human. She had hopes and dreams and a plan. And I knew all about going after what you wanted and putting it above everything else.

After all, I was the guy who still hadn't come clean to his old man about wanting Notre Dame over Michigan.

Scouts were coming out to the game Friday. I had to tell him before then. I had to rip off the Band-Aid and get it over with.

Yet, here I was, in Rixon Library of all fucking places, one second away from kissing the girl who'd betrayed me. Again.

"Avery?" she whispered again.

Fuck. My name on her lips did all kinds of things to me. Sinful things. Things I had no right wanting. It was senior year, the biggest year of my life. I didn't have time for girls, let alone ones as confusing and treacherous as Miley. And I knew she had her heart set on Northwestern. There was no point in starting something up with her when we both planned to leave next summer...

But: I. Couldn't. Stop. Thinking. About. Kissing. Her.

Maybe I just needed to get her out of my system? Yeah, that was it. Maybe I just needed some closure.

I stalked toward her, but Miley backed away. It didn't matter though. The invisible tether between us was undeniable, and it had only strengthened since school resumed.

All summer I'd tried to forget her, and then I'd taken one look at her on the first day of school and everything had come rushing back. But my feelings for her were confusing. Hatred woven with attraction. Disappointment tangled with desire. I wanted her. I wanted Miley in a way I'd never wanted anyone else, but I also couldn't forget what she'd done to me, to the team.

Fuck.

Her back finally hit the wall and I caged her in, pressing my hands on either side of her head. "W-what are you doing?" she murmured.

"Trying something." Leaning in, I ghosted my lips over hers, running my tongue over the seam of her lips. My heart crashed violently against my chest as her taste flooded my mouth.

"Avery..." Her voice was cracked with lust as she anchored her fingers in my hoodie and pulled me closer.

"Open up for me, Miley." *Let me in.*

She let out a soft sigh and I plunged my tongue into her mouth, burying one of my hands into her hair and stroking the side of her neck. Miley clutched me tighter, leaning up on her tiptoes to kiss me back. Hard and bruising, we fought for control, neither willing to bend.

"You taste so fucking good," I murmured the words as I slowed the kisses, teasing her.

"But what about Kendall?"

"Kendall?" Why the fuck did she keep mentioning Kendall?

"You want to talk about Kendall?" I nipped her bottom lip, soothing the sting with my tongue. "*Now?* When I'm thinking about doing very bad things to you?"

"Oh God," she breathed, as I slipped my hand underneath her t-shirt and splayed it over her stomach. Miley's skin was so warm and soft. I explored her body, reveling in the little moans she made as my hand found her breasts.

"We really shouldn't be doing this here," she whispered.

"Do you want me to stop?" I eased back to look at her. Her cheeks were flushed and eyelids heavy. She looked so fucking beautiful she stole my breath.

"N-no. God... no."

She was right. It was a risk, touching her like this in the library. The place where she worked. But it was like the rope had snapped, sending my control spiraling into oblivion.

I wanted her.

And it was all I could think about.

I trailed my fingers back down the flat of her stomach and dipped them inside her pants. Miley gasped, her entire body going tense.

"I-I've never—"

Fuck. She was a virgin.

Why did that make me even hotter for her?

"Shh." I kissed the corner of her mouth. "I've got you, just relax." Gently, I pushed a finger into her. She was so fucking tight. I didn't want to hurt her. But Miley didn't seem to care as she started to ride my hand.

"That feels..."

I circled her clit with my thumb, driving her wild. She tried to smother the little noises of pleasure crawling up her throat, but failed, so I kissed her hard, swallowing them for her.

"God, Avery... it's..." she moaned again.

"Come for me, babe... I need you to—" Miley's legs began to tremble as her orgasm crashed over her.

She buried her face in the crook of my shoulder, riding out the waves of pleasure. When she finally gave me her eyes again, she was wearing a shy smile.

"That was... unexpected."

Tell me about it, I internally groaned.

I gave her some space to tidy up. Miley tucked some strands of hair behind her ear and smiled at me again. "Is this the part where you tell me it was a mistake?" Her expression fell.

And I hated it.

I hated that she thought so lowly of me.

But I also hated that I lost control with her.

I was a fucking mess when it came to this girl.

"I see." Her lips pursed. "Well, I'll just be over there—"

"Wait." I snagged her wrist. "I'm just confused."

"About me?"

I nodded. "About what I feel for you. I thought if we got some closure—"

"That was supposed to be closure?" Lust and anger flared in her eyes and it made her look so damn cute, I wanted to kiss the shit out of her again.

"It wasn't." I admitted, and relief washed over her. "But I'm still confused. This, you and me, it's complicated."

Miley gave me a small nod. "I'll be at the desk when you're ready." This time when she walked away, I let her go. Because I needed space, and I couldn't think straight around her.

I copied the rest of my papers and made my way

over to the desk. The place was still empty, no signs of the manager.

"What time do you finish here?" I asked Miley.

"In thirty minutes. That's two dollars and fifty cents."

I dug out the money and paid her. "Thanks. Do you have a ride home?"

"No, I usually walk. It isn't far."

"I can give you a ride, if you want?"

"You don't have to do that, Avery."

"I want to," I said. "Please."

"Okay, I'd like that."

"Okay then, I'll wait outside."

———

WHEN MILEY finally exited the library, I was beginning to have second thoughts. This was a bad idea. My friends, the team... they wouldn't understand if I turned up tomorrow at school with Miley on my arm. She was the snitch. The girl who went against the Raiders. They wouldn't just overlook that, and I didn't want to give them any more ammunition to use against her. Not after what Micah, the fucking idiot, did to her at the party.

She gave me a small wave before making her way

over to my car. I leaned over and pushed the door open, and she climbed in.

"Are you sure this is okay?"

"I wouldn't have offered if I didn't want to." It came out harsher than intended and she frowned.

"Is everything okay?"

"No one will understand this," I said, letting out a frustrated breath.

"This?"

"Yeah. You and me. They won't get it. Not after what happened."

"Oh, I see." Miley folded her hands in her lap and stared down at them. "I didn't expect it to be easy, but people deserve a second chance, don't they?"

"Maybe. But my guys, the team... it's not that simple." Hell, even I couldn't forgive what she'd done.

So what the fuck was I doing here? Already imagining the next time I got to kiss her, to touch her and watch her fall apart.

"I don't know what to say. If I could do things differently, I would."

"What happened to doing whatever it takes to get to where you want to be?"

Her eyes lifted to mine. "I'm not saying I'd

have done everything differently, but I never wanted to hurt you, Avery. You have to believe me."

I nodded. It was all I could manage. The strange truth was, if Miley had never tried out for the cheer squad, I would never have gotten close to her. So it was only because of that damn exposé that our paths crossed. It was both a blessing and a curse, and that was a lot to reconcile.

We drove the short distance to her house in thick silence. I didn't doubt Miley was sorry for betraying me, but I still wasn't sure it could have ever played out any differently.

When I pulled up outside her house, she let out a resigned sigh. "I guess this is goodnight?"

"Guess so."

"And tomorrow when I see you at school?"

"Honestly," I said, "I don't know."

Dejection glistened in her eyes. "I guess I deserve that."

"Miley, this isn't me punishing you. It's not about that. But this season is a big deal for me. I have scouts coming to the game Friday. I have to tell my dad I don't want to apply to his alma mater. And everyone is expecting me to win State. I have a lot riding on my shoulders."

"And I'd just be another burden to carry. I get it. It's okay, Avery, you don't have to explain."

"That's not—fuck, why is this so hard?"

"It doesn't have to be. I guess you just have to figure out what you really want and what you're prepared to sacrifice to get it." She gave me a weak smile. "Goodnight, Avery, thanks for the ride."

Miley climbed out and slammed the door. The noise reverberated deep in my soul as I watched her walk up to her house. I wanted to go after her. I wanted to pull her into my arms and tell her I thought she was worth it. But something held me back.

Fear.

Guilt.

Shame.

There were too many fucking emotions vying for my attention and by the time I realized I needed to at least say goodnight to her, she was already gone.

———

THE HOUSE WAS quiet when I got home. I dropped my keys on the sideboard and kicked off my sneakers.

"Mom? Dad?" I called.

"In here, Ave."

My chest tightened. Coach had given me until yesterday to come clean and tell my dad the truth about Notre Dame. But I still hadn't found the words.

"Hey, Dad, what's up?"

"Sit. I think we need to talk, Son."

Shit. He knew. Coach had taken matters into his own hands and told him. Traitor.

I dropped into the seat and raked a hand through my hair. "Listen, I don't know what Coach told you, but I can—"

"Jase knows about this?" My dad's mouth curved. "Of course he does. But no, he didn't betray your confidence and tell me. I found the application."

"Oh."

"Why didn't you tell me?" His eyes narrowed with disappointment.

"I knew how badly you wanted me to go to Michigan, to follow in your footsteps. And I wanted it, Dad, I did. But then I started doing my research and Notre Dame reached out... and things changed."

"Jesus, Avery, you could have talked to me about this." He drummed his fingers on the table. "Was I excited about you following in your old man's footsteps? Hell yeah. I want this for you, Son, so freaking much. But I want you to want it too. And wherever you choose to go, I'll be there one hundred percent of the way."

"Really?"

"Of course." He chuckled. "I can't believe you thought you had to keep this from me."

It did seem kind of trivial now. But I knew what he'd given up when he chose our family over his dreams of going pro. I'd wanted to do this for him, to fulfil his dreams. But when it came down to it, I knew my heart wasn't in Michigan.

"I guess I didn't want you to see another one of your dreams go up in smoke."

"Avery," he shook his head gently, "that is not how I feel about it, you know that. I love my family more than anything. Do I wonder what life would have been like if things had gone differently? Sure, I do. But it wasn't meant to be. I might have lost my dream of football in senior year, but I gained something much, much better."

He reached across the table and laid his hand on mine. "I never want you to feel you can't come to me. Ever. I am always here, okay?"

"Thanks, Dad, and I'm sorry... I should have told you."

"Anything else you need to get off your chest?"

"Can I ask you something?"

"Anything."

"Back in high school, when you and Mom... you know."

"Yeah..." A faint smile traced his lips as if he was remembering.

"Gross."

"Hey, we were seniors once too."

"Don't remind me." I chuckled and he pinched my hand. "When you and Mom were sneaking around behind Coach's back, weren't you worried about betraying him?"

"I was." He scrubbed his jaw. "Jase is my best friend. I never wanted to hurt him. But how I felt about your mom, that wasn't something I could just turn off, Son. She saw me. She saw past the jersey and the team. She saw *me*. When you're in the kind of position you're in, Ave, that's a rare thing."

"So you were prepared to sacrifice your friendship with Coach for his sister?"

"*Step*-sister," he corrected me. "I guess. But what I really hoped was that if Jase valued our friendship as much as I did, then ultimately, in the end, he'd want us to be happy. Where is all this coming from, Son?"

"I just wondered." I shrugged, trying to school my expression.

"Wait a second, is there a girl on the scene? It wouldn't happen to be this Miss Fuller I've heard so much about from Jase would it?"

"Good talk, Dad," I got up.

Laughter rumbled in his chest. "Oh, don't be like that. You can talk to me about this stuff. I'm a cool dad. I'm down with the kids."

"Never going to happen, old man." Waving him off, I headed for the stairs.

A weight might have been lifted now my dad knew the truth about Notre Dame, but I still had the issue of what to do about Miley.

I knew I couldn't just turn off my feelings for her, not now.

But was I really prepared to risk everything to be with the girl who had betrayed the team?

The girl who betrayed me?

CHAPTER TEN

Miley

WHEN I ARRIVED at school on Wednesday morning, I didn't know what to expect. Avery had seemed so torn over what happened in the library. Part of me knew I was supposed to feel ashamed of letting him touch me like that in a public place, my workplace no less, but I didn't. Because the truth was, it had been one of the best few minutes of my life.

So when I saw him congregated in the quad with all his teammates and a few of the cheerleaders, my heart dropped. Because this is what he meant when he said it was complicated. Avery Chase was their captain, their leader. He wasn't supposed to date the head editor of the school newspaper, and he definitely wasn't supposed to date the girl who had betrayed the team.

Stuffing down my hurt, I made my way into school and headed straight for my locker. After retrieving the books I needed, I slammed it shut, almost jumping out of my skin when I realized Kendall Novak was standing beside it.

"I didn't see you there," I said.

"Too busy daydreaming?"

"Something like that," I mumbled.

"Dreaming of anyone in particular?" She smirked.

"Nope, can't say I was."

"You know Homecoming is right around the corner. You should come."

"It's not really my thing." My brows furrowed.

"But it could be. You could get a new dress, do your hair all pretty. Who knows, maybe someone might even ask you to go. On a... Real. Life. Date."

"What do you really want, Kendall?" I sighed, growing tired of her bullshit.

"Me? Nothing." She shrugged, twirling a strand of hair around her finger. "I'm just saying, you don't have to be such a bore all the time. You were kind of fun last year."

"Great, thanks. Now if you don't mind, I have to get to class." I went to move around her, but she blocked my path. "Think about it. We could double date... the four of us."

I froze, my breath catching in my throat.

Surely she didn't mean...?

"I thought that would get your attention." A wicked glint flashed in her baby blues. "It'll be fun. Me and Avery, and you and Micah. Or Ben. Or whoever. I'm sure Avery can get one of them to pity date you."

My cheeks burned as I realized everyone had stopped to watch the show.

"You're—you're going to Homecoming with Avery?" The words barely got out over the lump in my throat.

"Of course. He just asked me." She shrugged again. "Why? You didn't actually think he'd want to go... with *you*?" Her expression lit up with victory. "Oh my God, you did, didn't you? You actually thought that Avery would ask you."

School dances weren't my scene, but of course I'd thought about it. What sane girl wouldn't?

"I didn't..." I stuttered, trying to find the words. "Why would I think that?"

"Because, snitch, we've all noticed the way you

watch him when you think nobody is watching. You want him, admit it."

"I—"

"Hey, Miley." Lily Ford appeared, breaking the tension swirling around me and Kendall.

"What, are you two like friends now?"

"So what if we are?" I said.

"But you're a senior and she's in ninth grade."

"So?" Lily laced her arm through mine. It was a sweet gesture, one that made me feel all warm inside. But it was lost on Kendall. It was just more ammunition for her to hate me.

"You really are pathetic, you know that? You can't have Avery, so you figured you'd try to insert yourself into his life. Let me guess, you're friends with Ashleigh too?"

"So what if she is?" Ashleigh appeared, glowering at Kendall.

"I knew you were fucking weird, but this... this is something else. Does Avery know that you're trying to—"

"You should go before I call my brother and see exactly what he thinks about this." Ashleigh stared Kendall down despite being almost a head shorter than her.

"Ashleigh, it's okay," I said. "Kendall was just leaving, weren't you?"

"Yeah, I'm going. But you should watch your back with this one," she said, glancing at Lily and Ashleigh, "she'll betray you as soon as you turn around."

Kendall took off down the hall and everyone went back to what they were doing before she pulled the rug out from under my feet.

Avery had invited her to Homecoming.

How could he?

I guess it didn't matter now. He was right, nothing about us was easy. It was never going to be easy. He needed to focus on the team, the biggest season of his life, and I needed to stay in my lane and focus on getting accepted into Northwestern.

Maybe in another life, without the school newspaper and football we would stand a chance, but there were too many odds stacked against us.

"Are you okay?" Ashleigh asked.

"I'll be okay, thanks."

"She is such a bitch," Lily added. "What was she saying to you before we arrived?"

"It doesn't matter." I forced a smile. "I'm used to girls like Kendall."

"Was it true? What she said about my brother?"

"I'm not using you. I would never—"

"Not that," Ashleigh tsked, "I meant the other thing. That you want him."

"It doesn't matter." My heart ached. Last night in the library, Avery had given me a sign of hope. But in the harsh light of day, I knew it was only a fantasy.

"Of course it does. You can't give up just because of Kendall. She's—"

"Look, I appreciate your support, I do. Honestly, I think you're the first friends I've ever really had, and it has nothing to do with the fact you're Avery's family. But you need to let this go."

"But—"

"Leigh," Lily shook her head.

"Fine. But I still want you to come to Homecoming with us. My dad said we can go since we'll be hanging out with a senior." She grinned at me, and I felt myself soften.

"I'm still thinking about it." The last thing I wanted was to go to Homecoming and see Avery with Kendall, but how was I supposed to tell Lily and Ashleigh no when they had been nothing but kind to me?

"Well, I already got you a ticket, so you have to come."

"I'll see."

"You'll come." The corner of her mouth tipped.

"You sound awfully sure of yourself."

"Who, me? See you around, Miley. Lil." Ashleigh waved us off as she disappeared down the hall.

"Is she always so..."

"Weird?" Lily snickered.

"I was going to say confident."

"Ashleigh is the kind of girl who knows what she wants and goes after it. She's one of the best people I know."

"That's nice. I never really had that... a ride or die friend." I'd had friends over the years, sure. But never one that stuck. And once Dad left, I kind of just stopped trying.

I think that's why I'd fallen so easily for Avery.

I let out a resigned sigh.

"I know you messed up last year, Miley, with the exposé. But it isn't a reason to hide."

It was such a bold statement from the girl who I found cowering in the bathroom.

"How do you do it?" I asked quietly.

"Do what?"

"Pick yourself up like that?"

Lily looked at me and swallowed. "I've gotten really, really good at hiding things."

———

I MANAGED to avoid Avery for the rest of the day. But there was no avoiding him after school. Coach Ford had invited me to attend one of their meetings. I didn't really know what to expect, but when I stepped foot into the darkened room it didn't matter, because all I saw was him.

Avery was sitting forward in his chair, a Raiders ball cap pulled backward on his head, elbows propped on his thighs and chin nestled on his fists. He looked up and smiled, but it quickly fell when I didn't smile back.

Did he really think I was going to be okay with everything?

"Ah, Miss Fuller, glad you could join us. I thought it might be useful for you to join one of our strategy meetings."

"Where's everyone else?" I asked, noting only Avery was here.

"Typically, this is something we do with our QB when we have a big game coming up. The Eagles have a big defense, so we want Avery to know what to watch for, which players to avoid. But we also want to learn their weak spots, and tailor our plays to fit their strategy."

"Sounds complicated." I laughed, but it came out strangled.

"Studying film tape is all part of the process. It's how we learn and grow." Coach offered me a chair and I sat down, relieved I wasn't near Avery. It was bad enough being in the same room as him.

"You know, a little birdie told me you didn't come to the game last Friday."

"I... no, I didn't. I don't need to attend games to write the article."

"True," he said. "But we'd really like you to be there on Friday. It's our rival game against Rixon East and they always prove to be exciting."

"I'll... think about it."

"I've put a ticket aside for you."

"Thanks."

"Okay, let's get started." Coach pointed his remote at the tv screen and pressed the button. Footage of the Raiders rival team, the Rixon East Eagles filled the screen. I didn't know much about football, but even I knew about the bitter rivalry between our school and the high school across the river. It dated back decades, and there was no escaping rivals week.

Historically, both schools would prank each other in the lead up to the game, but that had been stamped out over recent years after a prank went wrong back in Coach Ford's days.

I watched quietly as Coach, Avery, and the assistant coaches paused the footage every few minutes and discussed play options, and defensive strategy. Coach made notes on a whiteboard, scribbling lines and circles and arrows that I recognized as play strategy, but I had no real idea what it all meant.

They seemed to forget I was even there, until forty minutes later, Coach flipped the light switch and startled me.

"Still with us, Miss Fuller?"

"Just about, sir." I smiled.

He chuckled. "Well, maybe it's given you a little insight into just what goes into game day."

I gave him a small nod.

"And think about the offer of that game ticket."

"I will, sir, thank you." I got up and moved to the door. "My report is due to Mr. Jones Monday, and then I'll be out of your hair."

"I look forward to reading it. Hopefully we've managed to change your mind a little about us." He went over to Avery and the other coaches and I slipped out of the room, inhaling a deep breath.

Coach Ford was insistent on making me see that

there was more to the team than just drunken parties, missed assignments, and cocky attitudes... but why? It didn't make any sense. Nothing had really changed because of my article. Sure, Principal Kiln and Mrs. Bennet were implementing stricter academic expectations of its star athletes, but eventually it would all fade away. I knew that, everyone knew that.

But he seemed so intent on changing *my* mind.

I threw my bag over my shoulder and started down the hall, but a voice stopped me.

"Miley, wait."

My heart lurched into my throat as I forced myself to turn around.

"I looked for you today," Avery said. "I wanted to talk to you about some—"

"It's fine," I rushed out. "We don't have to do this."

"We don't?" He frowned.

"No, I thought about it, and you're right. This, us, it could never work." My heart splintered. "Goodbye, Avery."

I walked away, and this time...

It was for good.

CHAPTER ELEVEN

Avery

"FEELING GOOD?" Ben asked me as I tied my cleats.

"Yeah, I'm ready."

It was game night and the biggest night of my life. Not only were we playing against Rixon East, our rivals, but the scouts from Notre Dame were also coming out to watch me.

"Look alive, ladies," Coach entered the locker room, and a ripple of anticipation went through the air. The crowd was electric above us, a constant rumble of applause as they made the various announcements.

"Chase, you with us, son?" Coach drilled me with a concerned look.

"I'm good, Coach."

"Glad to hear it. Tonight is your night to shine. Stick to the playbook and this game is ours." He clapped me on the shoulder, and I nodded.

I was ready.

More than ready.

But I couldn't shake the way things had been left between me and Miley. She'd given me no chance to explain, and then spent the rest of the week avoiding me. I knew Coach had asked her to come tonight, but I had no idea if she planned on it or not.

Not that it should have mattered.

"Okay, everybody in. Raiders on three."

"One... two... three..."

"Raiders." It echoed off the walls, reverberating through me, and fueling me for the battle ahead. The Eagles would come at us with everything they had, hoping to end our road to the championship before it even got started.

"Hell yeah." Micah grabbed my shoulder and leaped into the air. "Nothing like a little rivals game to get the blood pumping."

"Knock it off, asshole." I elbowed him in the ribs.

Things were still strained between us, but you couldn't go out onto the field with any bad blood between you and your teammates, not if you wanted to stay focused and win.

He laughed it off, moving ahead of me as we lined up to make our way onto the field. There was nothing like Friday night football. The glare of the lights, the anticipation of the crowd, the noise, right down to the smell of freshly cut grass. Stepping out onto that field was like coming home and for a second, everything went silent before zeroing in and exploding into heart pumping chaos.

"Ready?" Coach asked as I passed him. It was tradition that he followed us out.

"I think so." Blood roared in my ears, the rumble of the crowd growing beyond the doors.

"You've got this." He gripped my shoulder. "Whatever happens out there tonight, I'm proud of you, Avery. We all are."

"Thanks, Coach." I swallowed over the lump in my throat and grabbed my helmet. My future lay out there...

All I had to do was go out there and take it.

"OKAY, GET IN HERE." Coach called us in. It was the fourth quarter, and we were trailing behind the Eagles 34-29. The lead should have been ours, but a couple of bad decisions had swayed things in their favor.

"We've got a minute on the clock." He whipped off his blue and white Raiders ball cap and ran a hand through his dark hair. "This game should have been ours in the second quarter. But it doesn't matter. We leave all that at the door. We've got one minute on the clock. It's time to go big or go home. Chase, talk to me."

"There's only one play here, sir. You get me the ball and I'll get it to the end zone."

"That's what I like to hear, son. We run it, and you don't let go of that ball, son, not until you're over the line."

I nodded, anticipation firing off around my nerve endings. It was now or never. Forty-seven minutes of pushing hard all came down to this single play. If we converted, we'd win, if we didn't... well, that wasn't an option. I held out my hand and the assistant coach threw me a water bottle. I took a big gulp before squeezing the rest over my face.

"Raiders on three," Coach said, pushing his hand

into the middle of the huddle. Mine followed, then Ben's and Micah's, until the entire team was piled on top.

"One... two... three... Raiders."

The crowd cheered us back onto the field as we moved into position. My parents were in the crowd with Ashleigh and Uncle Xander, Coach's wife and daughters too. And I knew the Bennets would be here to cheer us on. Football wasn't just a hobby for our families, it was a way of life.

I pulled on my helmet and bit down on the mouth guard, checking the players on either side of me. It was a risky play, going for it on the fourth down, but we needed the touchdown.

"Blue fifty-two," I yelled. "Blue fifty-two."

Our center rocked on the balls of his feet, waiting for the whistle. The second it sounded, he snapped the ball to me, and I dropped back waiting for my running back to fake the pass. He took off to the left, drawing the eye of the Eagles defense while I put my head down and ran. My legs pumped as hard as they could as I ate up the yard markers. Thirty... twenty... ten...

A swarm of red and white hovered on the periphery of my sight but I had to trust my guys would take care of them. Until one lunged, landing right in front of me. I anticipated his fall and leaped into the air, just clearing his body. My feet hit the ground and I flew into the end zone, slamming the ball down.

"Touchdooooooown," the announcer's voice echoed around the stadium, drowned out by the roar of the crowd. My heart crashed violently against my chest as my teammates crowded me, cheering my name as if I was their messiah.

We'd done it.

We'd beaten our rivals and put on one hell of a show doing it. But as I looked around the crowd, all on their feet and celebrating our last-minute win, I found myself searching for only one face.

And she wasn't there.

———

"CHASE, GET OVER HERE," Coach yelled, and I jogged over to where he and a tall man wearing a Fighting Irish jacket stood.

"This is Mr. Drummond from Notre Dame."

"It's good to meet you, sir." I held out my hand and he shook it.

"Quite the game you played out there tonight."

"Thank you."

"Bold, aggressive, it's exactly the kind of talent we're looking to recruit for the Fighting Irish."

"Playing for Notre Dame would be a dream come true, sir."

"Glad to hear it, son." He pulled out his wallet and dug out a card, handing it to me. "I'll be in touch."

"That would be great, sir."

"You should go celebrate with the rest of your team, you've earned it." He clapped me on the shoulder, and I gave him a small nod.

"Hit the showers, Chase. I'll catch up with you later."

I left them to it and made my way through the tunnel leading to the locker room. The guys all cheered the second I walked inside.

"Yeah, yeah," I said. "It was one game. We still have eight to go," I reminded them.

"Nah, QB, we've got this." Micah pointed at me, winking.

I made quick work of showering, knowing that my family would be waiting outside to congratulate me. It was a post-game ritual that we would head to Bell's and eat together. Then they would go home while I went onto a party or to hang out with the guys.

The second I walked out of the stadium, my sister made a beeline for me. "You were amazing." She threw her arms around me.

"Thanks." I chuckled. Her enthusiasm for football never ceased to amaze me.

"You played a good game," Dad said, coming over. "Did the scout introduce himself?"

"Yeah."

"And?"

"He said he'd be in touch."

"Yes!" Dad pulled me in for a hug. "I'm so proud of you, Avery."

"Thanks, Dad."

"Okay, husband of mine, don't monopolize all his hugs."

We both laughed, looking over at Mom, who stared at me with so much pride in her eyes, I felt a little choked up.

"Congratulations, baby." She wrapped her arms around me. "You did good."

"I always do good, Mom."

"Yeah, baby, you do."

"Hey, where's Uncle Xander?"

A chill went through the air as my parents shared a glance.

"What?" I asked.

"Nothing," Dad smiled, but it didn't reach his eyes. "He's sorry he couldn't be here."

"Right."

"Well done, Ave," Poppy and Lily approached with their mom.

"Thanks."

"I bet Jason is so proud of you," their mom Felicity said.

"Damn straight he is." Coach stalked toward us. "But now he wants to eat." His eyes narrowed on his wife, glittering with hunger.

"Ew, Dad, gross," Poppy fake barfed.

"One day, Pops, one day you'll know how it feels," her mom chuckled.

"One day when she's much, *much* older."

"Like anyone would be brave enough to date me knowing you're my dad. I'm doomed."

We all laughed at that.

"Where's Asher?" Coach asked my dad.

"There was an issue with Ezra. They headed home."

"Well, I don't know about the rest of you," Dad

said. "But I'm ready for the meanest burger Bell's does."

———

"WHAT ARE YOU TWO WHISPERING ABOUT?" I hissed at Lily and Ashleigh. They hadn't stopped since we arrived at Bell's.

"Nothing," Lily rushed out a little too quickly. She shot my sister a hard look, but Leigh cleared her throat.

"Miley was at the game, you know?"

"She was?"

Ugh.

I internally groaned at the hope in my voice. Now my sister and Lily were staring at me with amusement in their eyes.

"I mean, that's cool."

"What the hell were you thinking, Ave?"

"Excuse me?" I said right as Lily nudged my sister in the ribs.

"She told us in confidence, Lil."

"Told you what?" That piqued my interest.

"Oh, you know, just what a jackass my brother is." Leigh arched her brow at me.

"Will you just tell me what the hell is going on?"

Miley was at the game?

Why didn't she wait around to see me?

Because she made it pretty clear she didn't want to see you again, asshole.

"Why'd you kiss her and then invite Kendall Novak to Homecoming? That was a real jerk move."

"*What?*" My brows furrowed. "I didn't invite Kendall to Homecoming."

"Well, she thinks you did. She told Miley that you were going together. Even suggested you could double date with Miley and Micah."

"What the fu—hell? I haven't even thought about Homecoming." I'd go. It was kind of expected. But I had no plans to take a date.

"So let me get this straight." I ran a hand down my face. "Miley thinks I'm taking Kendall to Homecoming?"

"Yep."

"And when did this all happen?"

"I think it was Wednesday."

Fuck. The same day Miley blew me off. No wonder she was acting weird. She thought I'd fooled around with her in the library and then gone to school the next day and asked Kendall to Homecoming.

"I didn't invite Kendall to Homecoming," I said.

"Well, duh." Leigh rolled her eyes, "That's what I told Miley. I told her you would never invite that bitch."

"Leigh," I warned.

"What? It's true. She was all up in Miley's face in the hall at school. Me and Lily jumped in to save her." She looked so damn pleased with herself.

"Fuck," I hissed under my breath. "And you didn't think to tell me this sooner?"

"Miley only really told us what happened tonight."

"Yeah, after you wouldn't let it go," Lily said.

Ashleigh shrugged. "I don't like seeing my friends miserable."

I fought a smile. That was typical Ashleigh. And I couldn't deny it soothed something inside me, knowing that Miley had my sister in her corner. Even if she was in ninth grade.

"I need to go," I said, shooting up from the table.

"Avery? What is it, Son?" Dad asked.

"I... uh, I need to..."

"There's a girl," Ashleigh said, and I shot her a *what the fuck* look.

"Let me guess, Miss Fuller?" Coach smirked.

"Wait a minute," I said, "you know about that?"

"I had my suspicions."

"But how?"

"Because, Avery, I was young once, and there's no escaping these women once they get their claws into you."

Well then.

I gawked at him like he'd grown a second head.

But then he gave me a serious look and said, "What are you waiting for, son? Go get your girl."

CHAPTER TWELVE

Miley

WHEN I GOT HOME, the house was empty. Mom had left a note on the refrigerator saying that she'd gone out with some girlfriends from work. It was a big deal, and I was so proud of her for trying to reclaim her life.

I grabbed a tub of ice cream from the freezer and a spoon and perched on one of the stools. There was nothing that cookie dough ice cream couldn't solve.

I shouldn't have gone to the game tonight. I knew that the second I watched Avery emerge from the tunnel with his teammates. God, he'd looked so good in his shoulder pads and tight white pants. I'm pretty sure I'd had actual drool. But then I'd watched Kendall cheering for him from the sideline and my stomach had dropped into my toes. They made the perfect couple. Cheerleader and football captain.

Girls like me didn't end up with guys like Avery. But I kept thinking back to the library. To the way he'd kissed me, the way he'd touched me. You couldn't just make up that kind of chemistry, could you? Because I felt it. I felt it every time I locked eyes with him.

It didn't matter anymore though. The article was done. I'd submitted it earlier. I had no more reasons to be following him or the team around. And Avery had an important season ahead.

Our paths were moving in two different directions.

It didn't make the pain any less though. I guess this was what heartache felt like.

I'd demolished almost half a tub of ice cream when a knock at the door startled me. Frowning, I slipped off the stool and went to answer the door.

"Avery?" My heart almost leaped out of my chest. "What are you doing here?"

"Can we talk?"

"You want to talk?" I didn't understand. "Don't you have somewhere more important to be?"

"Will you just invite me in, so I don't have to stand out here making a fool of myself?"

"Okay." I stepped aside, and he slipped past me.

Closing the door, I gave myself a second to compose myself. Avery was here, in my house, and he seemed so serious.

"Did something happen?" I asked, right as he said, "You were at the game?"

"I... yeah, I was at the game."

"Why?"

"Because Coach invited me, and your sister is really persuasive."

He chuckled at that. "Yeah, she is. Is that the only reason you came?" Avery watched me intently, his eyes pinning me to the spot.

"I... why are you here again?"

His lip curved. "You're cute when you're flustered."

"C-cute? What?"

"I didn't invite Kendall to Homecoming."

"You didn't?"

"No, I didn't." He stalked toward me, slipping his fingers into my belt loophole and tugging gently. I stumbled forward, my hands going to his chest to steady myself. He was so close, and I was so confused.

Avery was here, in my house, and he was looking at me like he wanted to kiss me again.

"Avery," I whispered. "What is happening right now?"

"I'm making a choice," he said.

"You are?" My mouth went dry.

"Yeah. You, Miley, I choose you." He leaned down, ghosting his lips over mine. "Is this okay?"

I nodded, not trusting myself to speak.

Sliding his hand into my hair, Avery pulled me closer and kissed me. My fingers twisted into his t-shirt as his tongue curled around mine.

"Is this real?" I breathed.

"Does this feel real?" His hand glided down my spine and pushed gently, fitting my body against his. I felt him hard and ready at my stomach.

"Oh..." Heat exploded in my cheeks.

"We don't have to—"

"No, I want to." I cupped his face, my heart galloping inside my chest like a band of wild horses. "I want you, Avery Chase."

"Yeah?" He gulped.

"Yeah." I smiled, hardly able to believe this was happening. "My mom is out. She won't be home for a while."

The air turned thick around us.

"Come on." I took his hand and led him upstairs to my bedroom. My body hummed with nervous energy. I'd never had a boy inside my bedroom before, let alone a boy like Avery.

"I feel like there's so much I don't know about you," he said, snagging me around the waist and pulling me back into his arms. His chin went to the crook of my neck and he kissed me there. "I want to know you, Miley, all of you."

My heart soared. He felt it too.

"I want that too, so much."

"But first, I really, really want to touch you again." His hand slid up my stomach, taking my t-shirt with it. Warm fingers tickled my skin, moving higher until he grazed the shell of my bra. "You're so soft," he whispered, nipping my ear.

A delicious shudder rolled through me. "Avery." I pressed my lips together, smothering the whimper building in my throat.

"What do you want? Tell me."

"Touch me, please."

A wildfire burned through me. I wanted his hands all over me, touching and teasing.

"Patience," he chuckled.

Avery released me and slowly pulled my t-shirt off. Every time his fingers brushed my skin, I shuddered. Then his hands went to my leggings and pushed them over my hips. I shimmied out of them and he picked me up, my shrieks filling the room.

"Put me down," I batted his chest. He dropped me on the bed, crawling over me, pulling off his t-shirt as he went. I wrapped my arms around his broad shoulders, leaning up to kiss him.

"What made you change your mind?" I asked.

Avery brushed the hair out of my face as he stared down at me. "I've spent my entire life going after what I want. And then you came along and knocked me on my ass. I fell hard for you, Miley. I just didn't know what to do about it. And then I kissed you and you pulled away... When that shit followed with the exposé. I was so fucking angry."

"I'm so sorry. You have to know—"

"I get it. I think that's what I hate the most. I know what it's like to want something so much you'll do anything to make it happen. We're the same, Miley. I see that now. And I'm not about to let you slip through my fingers just because I got my feelings hurt."

"I'm still sorry. By the time I realized how I felt about you... it was too late. I—"

"Shh." He pressed his thumb to my lips. "It doesn't matter. All that matters is this moment."

"And Monday when school rolls around?" I hated how insecure I sounded, but he'd said it himself, no one would understand.

"Simple. I'm going to pick you up and we're going to walk into school together."

"They won't understand."

"They don't have to. I'm Avery fucking Chase. If I want to date the geek from the school newspaper, then I will." His lips curved with amusement.

"Did you just refer to me as a geek?"

"Yeah, *my* geek." He leaned down, brushing his nose along mine before kissing me.

"I think I like the sound of that."

We fell into the kiss. Avery took his time learning all the ways to make me sigh and squirm. His fingers explored my skin, painting letters of love on my ribs and gently squeezing my breasts.

When I was a ball of tightly sprung energy, he finally dipped his fingers inside my panties and touched me where I needed him most.

"I can't wait to be inside you," he rasped, watching me as he curled his fingers deeper, rolling his thumb over my clit.

"Oh God," I cried.

My fingers twisted into the bed covers as the

waves of pleasure rose inside of me. "Kiss me," I breathed. "I need you to kiss me."

Avery chuckled, diving at me and capturing my lips in a hard kiss. His tongue plunged into my mouth, swallowing the moans crawling up my throat. "Come for me, Miley."

His words send me hurtling over the edge, my body splintering apart.

Avery kissed me again before rolling off me to remove his jeans. He grabbed a condom from his wallet and came back to the bed. "Are you sure?"

I nodded, watching with rapt fascination as he ripped open the foil packet with his teeth and sheathed himself.

He covered my body, sliding his hand under one of my thighs and hitching it around his waist. "This might hurt." Avery rocked into me slowly, inch by inch. My breath caught at the sudden fullness, but the pain quickly gave way to pleasure as he began moving inside me.

"You are so fucking beautiful." He ran his thumb down my cheek and let it linger on the pillow of my lip before replacing it with his mouth.

"I can feel you everywhere," I whispered, clinging to him as I tried to catch my breath.

"Fuck, Miley..." He dropped his lips to my throat and sucked gently.

My hands ran over his shoulders and down his back. I could feel every muscle, every dip and plane. He was a work of art, sculpted from years of dedication to football.

"You feel incredible." His teeth grazed my shoulder, sending shockwaves rippling through me.

He slipped his hand between us, rubbing my clit in lazy circles. Liquid lust coursed through my veins as I felt another wave build inside me.

"Avery..." I cried.

"Just let go, babe. I got you."

The rope snapped and my body shuddered around him. Avery swallowed my moans, lapping at my mouth with his tongue. He went faster, chasing his own release. The second he crashed over the edge, he kissed me, my name an echo on his tongue.

We lay there in the aftermath, sated and silent.

"Are you okay?" he asked me.

"Yeah. That was..."

How did I even begin to explain to him what I felt in this moment?

Avery touched his head to mine and smiled. "I know. Everything you felt. I felt it too."

Relief slammed into me. This wasn't some joke or cruel revenge plan... it was real.

And it was more than I could have ever hoped for.

———

"SWEETHEART, you're going to burn a hole in the carpet," Mom said as I paced the living room. "He'll be here."

"I know." I did.

Avery had already texted me three times to say he'd see me soon. But it was Monday morning, and I was so freaking nervous about walking into school as his girlfriend.

Avery Chase's freaking girlfriend.

I still couldn't believe it.

We'd spend most of the weekend together. He'd met my mom Saturday and then I'd been over to his house yesterday to meet his parents.

It was moving fast. But Avery said we'd wasted too much time already, and I was inclined to agree.

But school?

School was a whole other deal.

"I think I see his car," Mom clapped, unable to keep the excitement out of her voice.

I wasn't sure she'd be so excited if she knew what we'd been up to in my room Saturday night, but what she didn't know couldn't hurt her. Besides, I was almost eighteen.

It still amused me that I was older than Avery. He didn't turn eighteen until next spring, but there was nothing boyish about the way he made me feel or the dirty things he did to me.

"Okay, sweetheart, this is it."

"Please, Mom. I'm already nervous enough."

"You've got this, baby. I'm so proud of you. You and Avery make such a cute couple. Don't let anyone tell you any different, okay?"

"Thanks, Mom." I hugged her. "For everything."

"Oh, sweetheart, it's me who should be thanking you. I don't know what I would have done without you these last couple of years."

There was a knock at the door and my heart catapulted into my throat.

"That's him," Mom shrieked.

"Oh my God, Mom, stop." I waved her off as I grabbed my bag and went to the door. "Hey," I said to Avery, trying to play it cool.

"Hey?" His brows crinkled. "Get over here." He pulled me into his arms and kissed me thoroughly.

"What was that for?" I asked, my cheeks burning.

"I missed you. Morning, Ms. Fuller."

"Good morning, Avery. Now you drive safe, okay?"

"I will, ma'am."

"Okay then, off you two go. And 'Go Raiders.'"

"Oh my God," I murmured, "make it stop."

"I think it's cute." Avery grabbed my hand and pulled me toward his car. "Ready?" He opened the door for me, but I hesitated.

"Miley... we're doing this. Together, okay?"

"I know," I flashed him a weak smile and climbed into his car.

Before I changed my mind.

———

"YOU'VE GOT to get out eventually," Avery said. We'd been sitting in his car for five minutes.

"I know, I just need another minute."

"Babe," he grabbed my hand across the center console, "what's the worst that can happen?"

"Seriously?" I balked. "Have you met Kendall?"

"Kendall will fall in line because I'll tell her to fall in line. I think you're forgetting one key thing here. I'm a god in this place. What I say goes. You have nothing to worry about."

"Did you just refer to yourself as a god?"

"*That's* what you're choosing to take from everything I just said?" He smirked and I pinched his hand. "Oh look, the cavalry has arrived."

"The cav—"

Ashleigh knocked on the window. "Come on," she mouthed. "I can't wait to see Kendall's face."

"Oh my God," I chuckled. "Your sister is—"

"An idiot? Yeah, I know."

"Actually, I think she's pretty awesome."

"Well, I think you're pretty awesome. Now can we please get out of the car?"

"Okay." I shouldered the door and Ashleigh and Lily backed up to give me some space.

"Thank God. I thought you were going to sit in there all morning."

"Hey, Ashleigh, good to see you too."

"Aaaand here we go." She let out a low whistle and I immediately saw the reason. Everyone had stopped to watch me climb out of Avery's car.

He came around to my side and grabbed my hand. "Just breathe, babe. I got you."

"They're all staring."

"Yep. That's what happens when you're dating

the star quarterback who never dates." Ashleigh smirked.

"Leigh," Avery warned.

"What, I'm just saying."

"You good?" He squeezed my hand.

Avery seemed so calm and composed. Why did he seem so calm and composed?

"Yo, Chase, man." Micah sauntered over to us. "I was going to ask what you were doing all weekend but looks like I have my answer."

"Don't be a dick," Avery warned.

"Snitch, looking good." Micah's mouth curved, but I saw no contempt there.

"I guess you don't look bad either, for an asshole."

Avery exploded with laughter as I smothered a smirk of my own.

"Touché, Miley. Tou-fucking-ché. Guess I'll spread the word that the snitch just got bumped to QB's girl." He took off toward the school building.

"What just happened?" I asked Avery, dumbfounded.

He pulled me into his arms and tucked a flyaway strand of hair behind my ear. "You underestimate us, babe."

"But—"

"No buts. I'm going to kiss you now, okay?"

He didn't wait for my answer, cupping my face and kissing me deeply. Ashleigh and Lily made fake gagging noises, but they were soon drowned out when Avery's tongue curled around my own.

Until Ashleigh grumbled, "Bitch alert."

I eased back and glanced over to where Kendall was sending me an icy death stare.

"Ignore her," Avery said. But I didn't want to ignore her.

I wanted to make sure she knew exactly how things were.

So I kissed Avery again, just to make sure she got the message.

———

"WATCH IT, SNITCH." Kendall narrowed her eyes, contempt rolling off her, as she and her friends passed me in the hall.

It had been the same all morning. I tried not to let their whispers and taunts affect me, but I couldn't deny the confidence I'd felt kissing Avery outside of school slowly began to crack.

"I can't believe he's actually with her," she said a

little too loudly. "Unless it's all some joke to get her back for what she did last year."

Pressing myself to my locker, I shrunk into myself. If they hated me before, they really hated me now.

"Hey," Ashleigh strolled up to me. "Why are you hiding in here?"

"Not hiding, just... catching my breath."

"You cannot let Kendall Novak win." She gently coaxed me from my locker and slammed it shut. "My brother wants you, Miley. *You.*"

Her wide smile and kind words eased the knot in my stomach. "You know, you're pretty awesome."

"I know." She grinned proudly. "Now, no more hiding."

"Easier said than done," I murmured.

Micah had kept them at bay in my last class, but I still had a lot of classes to get through. Just then, my cell phone vibrated.

"Is it Ave?" Ashleigh peered over my hands and I snatched it away.

CAN'T MEET **you at lunch, I have practice. Sorry. But if you come and watch me after**

school, I'll give you a ride home?

"WHAT DID HE SAY?"

"He's got practice at lunch."

"Good thing you have me and Lily then." She grinned again.

"Good thing indeed." I looked up and Kendall glowered at me.

"Ignore her. Come on." Ashleigh gently tugged my arm.

I wanted to take her advice, but something told me Kendall wasn't going to take it easy on me. Because I had what she wanted.

I had Avery.

———

I SURVIVED the rest of the day. Thankfully, I only had one more class with Kendall, but I sat in a row behind her so she couldn't exactly keep turning around to taunt me.

The second I filed out of the room, Ashleigh and Lily pounced on me. "This is a surprise," I said.

"We thought we'd keep you company while Avery is at practice."

"Oh, okay." My brows furrowed.

But the second we made it to the bleachers, I realized why they had offered to come with me. The cheer squad was also practicing, and we had to walk right past them.

"Why would Avery really want her when he could have me?"

"I don't know, Kendall. They looked pretty serious this morning," her friend said, shooting me an apologetic look.

"Well, I'll be crowned Homecoming Queen. And everyone knows Avery will be King. There's no stopping destiny."

"God, she's so deluded," Ashleigh hissed as we moved around the squad to sit up in the bleachers.

I tried to block out Kendall and her venomous words and focus on Avery. He looked so good running drills. I had to pinch myself a couple of times, hardly able to believe he was mine.

But then Kendall caught my eye, smirking, and a sinking feeling spread through me. She would be crowned Homecoming Queen and Avery would be crowned King. And I didn't even have plans to go to the stupid dance.

The end of practice approached, and Coach

called the team into the huddle. But when they broke formation, I frowned.

"What are they doing?" A couple of players were jogging toward the bleachers holding their Rixon Raiders game night banner between them.

"Oh my God," Lily breathed as my eyes spelled out the words painted over the familiar Rixon Raiders lettering.

Miley Fuller, will you go to Homecoming with me?

"GO..." Ashleigh nudged me. "Go down there."

"I..." My heart crashed against my chest,

"Go." She yanked me up and gave me a gentle shove. I stumbled down the bleachers in a daze.

What the hell was going on?

I was aware of the entire cheerleading squad watching me as I made my way to the edge of the football field. Micah winked at me, nodding behind him. Then Avery burst through it, coming to a stop in front of me.

Everyone started cheering: his teammates, most

of the cheer squad, Lily and Ashleigh in the bleachers. Even Coach Ford was clapping.

"So, will you?" Avery took my hands in his.

"I..."

He leaned in, brushing the hair away from my face. "The answer is yes, Miley."

"Yes," it spilled out on a soft sigh. "Yes, I'll go to Homecoming with you."

How could I deny him after this?

"She said yes!" He roared, and the applause got louder.

"Oh my God, stop." I buried my face in his chest. But Avery cupped the back of my neck and gently lifted my face to his.

"I've never been to a school dance," I confessed, feeling my cheeks turn pink.

"Good," he said around a smile. "I want all your firsts, Miley. Every single one."

Avery captured my lips in a bruising kiss, one I felt all the way down to the tips of my toes.

My hands wound into his jersey. "Everyone's looking," I breathed.

"Good, let them watch. You're mine, Miley. And I'm never letting you go."

EPILOGUE

Miley

I WAS AT HOMECOMING... Homecoming.

I'd never been to a school dance before. But it was everything I expected a school dance to be. Loud, rowdy, and full of kids all looking to let loose, hook up, and make mistakes.

"Oh my God, you look amazing," Ashleigh and Lily found me while Avery was off getting us some drinks. Drinks he assured me would be alcohol-free. But I didn't trust Micah not to try and spike the punch.

"Thanks, my mom chose it." She'd insisted on taking me dress shopping. The Raiders-blue skater dress wasn't over the top or a showstopper, but I felt comfortable and Avery's eyes had lit up when he'd seen me. So I figured it was a winner.

"Well, you look great."

"So do you. Both of you." I winked at Lily. She looked completely out of her depth, eyes wide and full of fear. I still didn't know her whole story, but Lily Ford was a girl afraid of the world and it was such a freaking shame because she was all kinds of awesome.

"Here you go." Avery slipped his arm around my waist and handed me my drink.

"You clean up good, Ave," Ashleigh said, with a proud smile.

"I try."

"The game was incredible by the way. If Notre Dame don't want you, they're idiots."

"Thanks for the vote of confidence, brat." He gave me a knowing look. He hadn't told his family yet that he'd already verbally committed to them. It was a surprise.

"Wait a minute," Ashleigh said, glancing between us. "You know something, don't you?"

"You're too damn smart for your own good," he muttered.

"So... did you?"

"Did I what?" Avery smirked, and I buried my face against his shoulder, smothering my laughter.

"Oh my God, they want you, don't they?" Ashleigh shrieked. "Notre Dame totally wants you."

"Yeah, they do."

"Avery!" Ashleigh flung herself at her brother, almost knocking me out of the way. I stepped aside, letting them have this moment. "I'm so freaking proud of you. Mom and Dad are going to kill you when you tell them."

"I just wanted some time to process."

"Congratulations, Avery, that's amazing news," Lily said.

"Thanks. But I'd appreciate it if you let me tell Mom and Dad."

"I can keep a secret." Ashleigh zipped her lips. His brow went up and we all chuckled.

"Uh oh, here comes Principal Kiln."

My stomach lurched. I was dreading this part.

"Relax," Avery whispered against the shell of my ear. "Even if she wins,"—which we all knew she would—"I'm here with you, not Kendall."

"I know."

Kendall had spent all week trying to intimidate me. I tried to ignore her, but it wasn't always easy.

She was great at playing on every insecurity I had about myself and my relationship with Avery.

"Students, teachers, and friends," Principal Kiln's voice echoed through the room, "welcome to Homecoming." Cheers exploded around us, everyone chanting *Raiders, Raiders*. Avery gave the crowd a small salute but didn't let go of my hand as we stood there, surrounded by his teammates and friends. Ashleigh cast me a reassuring smile, and I managed a small one in return. I never imagined I'd find myself here, but I didn't want to be anywhere else.

"I'll keep this brief as I'm sure you all want to enjoy your evening. Please give it up for this year's Homecoming King and Queen, Mr. Avery Chase and Miss Kendall Novak."

Even though I knew it was going to happen my heart still sank.

Avery cupped my face and stared at me intently. "I'll be right back, okay?"

"Okay. Congratulations."

His lip quirked. "You say that like this means anything. It doesn't."

Ashleigh slid her hand into mine and squeezed gently.

"Go," I said to Avery. "They're waiting."

He hesitated but then melted into the crowd. Kendall was first on stage, eagerly accepting her tiara. She smiled like the cat who got the cream, especially when Avery reached the stage and accepted his crown. Lacing her arm through his, she beamed.

"What a deluded bitch," Ashleigh hissed.

But there was no denying how good they looked together.

"It's customary for the King and Queen to have one dance together," Principal Kiln added, "if you would like to make your way to the dance floor."

"I'm going to go to the bathroom," I whispered, trying to untangle myself from Ashleigh. But she tightened her grip on me.

"No, you are not."

"Ashleigh, please. I just need to—"

"Actually, Principal Kiln, I'm afraid that's not going to work for me."

I froze at the sound of Avery's voice.

"I-it's not?" The principal stuttered.

"No. You see, there's only one girl I'll be dancing with tonight, and that's my girlfriend, Miley Fuller."

Kendall's expression turned murderous as Avery lifted a hand to his face and searched for me in the crowd.

"I see. Well, I guess there's nothing that says you have to dance together. Kendall, do you perhaps have a date you can—"

But she stormed off the stage with a face like thunder.

"That was so freaking cool," Ashleigh whisper-shrieked.

"What do you say, Miley?" Avery said with conviction. "Will you dance with me?"

The room was silent save for the wild beat of my heart. Ashleigh gave me a small nudge forward and the crowd parted, leading me right toward Avery. He came off stage and stood before me. He looked so freaking handsome in his slacks and black shirt.

"You're not wearing your crown," I said.

"Don't need it." He shrugged. "Not when I have a much better prize waiting for me."

"You do?" I glanced around, making a show of looking for something.

"Miley." He banded his arm around my waist and pulled me close. "Stop."

"Okay," I breathed. "Is this the part where we dance?" I was vaguely aware of a song playing in the background.

"This is the part where I tell you how crazy I am about you."

"You are?"

Avery moved closer, brushing his nose over mine. "I am. I've fallen hard…" He swallowed, his eyes darkening.

"I guess it's a good thing I've fallen hard too then, isn't it?"

"Yeah?" He grinned.

"Yeah," I said.

And then I kissed him.

Avery

"Here he is," Coach said, welcoming me into his house. "The man of the hour."

"Thanks, Coach. Couldn't have done it without you."

"You're damn right there, kid." He smirked. "Miley, it's good to see you. I hope you're keeping this one out of trouble."

"I try." She squeezed my hand.

It was the Sunday after Homecoming and I'd finally told my parents about Notre Dame yesterday. I knew Ashleigh wouldn't be able to keep a secret and I wanted the news to come from me.

"Well, come on in, everyone's already here."

We followed Coach into his huge open plan

kitchen. My parents were standing with Felicity over at the counter. Mrs. Bennet and Asher were here too. I spotted the twins sitting outside around the fire pit with Lily, Poppy, and my sister.

"No Ezra?" I asked.

The Bennets shared a look. "He's... not feeling so good. Congratulations, Avery. We're all very proud of you."

"Thanks, Mrs. Bennet."

"Oh please, we're not in school now. You can call me Mya."

"Son." Dad approached me, pulling me into a hug. "She's right. We're proud, kid. So fucking proud."

"Cameron!" Mom gasped, and everyone chuckled.

"It's not every day your kid commits early to one of the best football programs in the country, Hailee. I think I'm allowed to get a little emotional."

"You can get emotional without the cussing."

"This looks great, you guys." I changed the subject, glancing over at the huge spread of food Coach and his wife had laid out for me.

"Well, it's a great reason to celebrate. Now all we need is to bring home that championship and my work here is done." Coach smirked again.

"No pressure then." I chuckled.

"You'll do it, babe." Miley leaned over and kissed my cheek and I swear all the moms in the room swooned.

"You two are just the cutest, and so lucky to be attending schools a stone's throw from each other."

"Oh, I won't hear back from Northwestern until the spring," Miley said.

"No, but you'll get in." She had to. Because spending four years without Miley close was not an option.

"I'm sure it'll all work out." Mom smiled.

They'd been so great about everything. Notre Dame. Miley. It had only been a couple of weeks since we walked into school that morning and surprised everyone, but I couldn't imagine life without Miley now. Some of the guys didn't get it. She was still a traitor in their eyes. But her second article had gone some way to repairing the damage done.

Micah had surprised me the most. He gave the word that Miley was my girl and that was that. If anyone had a problem with it, he took it upon himself to set them straight. I think it was his way of apologizing for what went down at his party. And maybe because he'd always suspected there was something between us.

Either way, things were good.

Better than good. Life was pretty fantastic.

Lily was doing better at school. Ashleigh was as annoying as ever. The team was on a winning streak. And I had the girl of my dreams by my side.

I had everything I needed.

And I couldn't wait to see what the future held.

THREE YEARS LATER...

Lily

"Hey, you," Mom joined me outside. I was curled up on a garden lounger, reading a book.

"Hey, Mom."

"How are you feeling?"

"Okay, I guess."

"You know, school starts in a week."

"I know." As if I could forget. It was senior year.

It only felt like two seconds ago, I was starting Rixon High as a shy ninth grader.

"You've come so far, baby. I have good feelings about this year."

"It'll be fine, Mom." It was my go-to response when things started to feel too much.

I'm fine.

It's fine.

Everything will be fine.

Mom knew, they all did. But they didn't push. I think over the years, it had gotten easier *not* to push. To just let me be.

"Has Dad found out what's happening yet?"

"He's on a conference call with Principal Kiln and Principal Mendoza right now. But whatever happens, I'm sure it'll be fine." She leaned over and squeezed my knee.

Over the summer, there had been a fire at Rixon East High School. Luckily no one was injured, but the damage was too extensive to repair in time for the new school year. The school board decided that kids would be shipped to the three nearest schools, including Rixon High.

It was all Ashleigh and Peyton, my best friends, had talked about all summer. I guess it was a big deal. Kids from Rixon East and Rixon High didn't exactly mix. The rivalry wasn't as bad as it was back in my dad's day, but there was no love lost between our two high schools.

"Sucks to be them," I said.

"Lil," Mom warned.

"What?" I shrugged.

She rolled her eyes. "Remember how you felt starting Rixon High in ninth grade? I imagine it's going to be scary and unknown for a lot of kids. A little compassion would go a long way, baby."

I didn't have the heart to tell her, that it wasn't them I was worried about.

It was me.

I could already feel the gnawing teeth of anxiety closing in around me. But I'd been doing so much better, and Mom and Dad were finally loosening the strings and giving me more freedom. I didn't want to ruin everything.

So I smiled and ignored the little voice in my head.

Everything would be fine.

Just then, Dad came outside and headed toward us.

"Uh oh," Mom said. "He looks pissed."

His eyes were narrowed, and his jaw was clenched. Oh yeah, my dad was definitely pissed.

"What did they say?" Mom leaped up.

"It's a fucking mess." He glanced over me and grimaced. "Sorry, Lil."

I waved him off.

"Since we're the better football program they want to transfer all their best players here. But like I told Principal Kiln, I already have a full roster."

"Well, I'm sure you'll make it work." She rubbed his shoulders. "They lost everything, Jase. It's the right call."

"Yeah, I know." He blew out a long, steady breath. "But Kaiden Thatcher is on that list."

"Lewis Thatcher's son?" Mom frowned, her expression darkening. "I see."

"Who's Lewis Thatcher?" I asked.

"No one you need to worry about, Lil," he said.

But his face said otherwise. His face said Lewis Thatcher *was* someone to worry about.

Which probably meant, his son was too.

PLAYLIST

Hopeless – Halsey, Cashmere Cat
Worst of You – Maisie Peters
Monster – Shawn Mendes ft. Justin Bieber
Dandelions – Ruth B.
Everybody Loves You – Charlotte Lawrence
Skin – Sabrina Carpenter
Wonder – Shawn Mendes
Collide – Rachel Patten

ACKNOWLEDGMENTS

I am SO excited to be back in the Rixon world, and I hope you enjoyed a little taster of things to come. Lily, Poppy, Ashleigh, Sofia, Aaron, Ezra, and Xander have so much coming your way, I hope you're ready!

Huge thanks to my beta team: Nina, Annissia, Heather, Cassie, and Amanda for all their input. To Darlene and Athena for fitting me in for a last minute proofread. To Andie, Tracy, and Anna for keeping me sane during these strange times we live in.

And a huge shoutout to every blogger, bookstagrammer, and reader who fall in love with my OG Raiders and gave me the encouragement to move onto their kids' stories. I really hope I do them justice.

Until next time,
    L A xo

ABOUT THE AUTHOR

Angsty. Edgy. Addictive Romance

Author of mature young adult and new adult novels, L A is happiest writing the kind of books she loves to read: addictive stories full of teenage angst, tension, twists and turns.

Home is a small town in the middle of England where she currently juggles being a full-time writer with being a mother/referee to two little people. In her spare time (and when she's not camped out in front of the laptop) you'll most likely find L A immersed in a book, escaping the chaos that is life.

L A loves connecting with readers.

The best places to find her are:
www.lacotton.com

Printed in Great Britain
by Amazon